"I'm good at massages," Amelia said. "Turn over and I'll show you."

Obediently, Sarah rolled facedown.

"Let's take this off." Amelia tugged at Sarah's shirt, pulling it out of her slacks.

Unbuttoning the blouse, Sarah shrugged out of it, then placed her face on her crossed arms. Stiffening as Amelia undid her bra and straddled her hips, her muscles turned to jelly when strong fingers climbed her spine.

"These too," Amelia said, snapping her waistband.

Raising herself, Sarah unzipped her pants and helped Amelia work them over her hips. Warmth flooded her.

"You have a nice body," Amelia said, gently kneading her behind, touching her intimately as if by accident.

She lifted herself to allow entrance. Excited, she moved against the long, slender fingers drawing pleasure from her.

Visit

Bella Books

at

BellaBooks.com

or call our toll-free number

1-800-729-4992

Seasons of the Heart

By

Jackie Calhoun

Bella
BOOKS

2005

Bella Books, Inc.
P.O. Box 10543
Tallahassee, FL 32302

First published 1997 by Naiad Press

Printed in the United States of America on acid-free paper
First Edition

Editor: Lila Empson
Cover designer: Bonnie Liss (Phoenix Graphics)

ISBN 1-59493-030-9

For Diane

Prologue

Sarah lay in the bed she'd shared with Fran these past five years and pretended to read. She had made up her mind to leave, was waiting for the opportune moment to tell Fran. She wasn't sure Fran even guessed at her restlessness. Looking over at her, she was surprised to see her awake.

"Want to make love?" Fran asked.

"Not tonight," she said. Not when she was struggling to be free.

"I remember when you couldn't keep your hands

1

off me." Fran's eyes turned a darker blue. "When you had so much to say to me."

She frowned a little. "I still do."

"No, you don't. You keep your thoughts to yourself. We seldom make love."

It was true, but Sarah couldn't point a finger at the reason. Her mother's death. Fran's mother's dying brain. Her own dead-end job. The sameness of everything. Their ritual vacations — the lake up north in the summer, Door County in the spring and fall, Winter Park for cross-country skiing in the winter, annual visits to Fran's children. Was that all there was ever going to be? The two of them going to work and coming home, vacationing at the same places, getting older without benefit of change.

"Are you happy, Fran?" she asked.

"We used to have so much fun together."

They had delighted in each other's company up till last winter. Maybe she just needed time away from work, from Fran, from the tediousness of routine. "It's late." She turned off the bed lamp and stretched out, turning her back to Fran. Humid air drifted through the open window.

Fran moved close and put an arm around her.

"It's too hot, Fran."

"I love you, Sarah."

"I love you too." It wasn't a lie. She had never loved anyone else as she did Fran. There was no one else in her life — just an emptiness that made her desperate.

When Fran began crying quietly, she scooped her close. "Shh. Don't." This wasn't fair. It was time to either move on or mend the relationship. But she found she couldn't go backward.

2

I

Flat and steely gray, the lake reflected the clouds mounding overhead. Fran stood at the sloping boat ramp in the August heat, blinking the sweat out of her eyes. Hands on hips, she moved in place to relieve her cramping calf muscles. The rasping struggle to breathe had eased, although her chest heaved, reminding her that she was not a runner. Shading her eyes, she squinted at the boat distancing itself, its white wake widening.

Fuck, fuck, fuck. The truck and trailer had passed her on the road, causing her to break into a trot.

3

She imagined Sarah hurrying to unload the bass boat, parking the truck and trailer across the road, then rushing back to push off. She hoped the rain started soon and drove her off the lake.

Feeling sick inside, shaking outwardly, she turned away. When Sarah returned, she would ask her, *Why didn't you wait? You knew I wanted to go with you.*

But she knew Sarah would reply, *I wanted to be alone.* And mean it.

Dispiritedly, she scuffed through rutted sand to the blacktop. It was hot for a Wisconsin summer, suffocating even without the sun. The first raindrop struck her forehead, a cool surprise. Another splat was followed by half a dozen more and then a deluge. She found refuge under a huge white pine that smelled strongly of resin. Sitting at its base, she leaned against the trunk and watched sheets of rain sweep by in gusts.

Across the road, Sarah's truck steamed. A bent figure raced across the blacktop, unlocked the door, and jumped inside. The truck and trailer backed around in a wide curve, straightened, and headed toward the boat ramp.

Fran followed. When the trailer was backed into the lake, she walked up behind Sarah and asked, "Want some help?"

Sarah was winching the boat onto the trailer and apparently hadn't seen or heard her approach. She jumped, making Fran wonder if she hadn't driven past her on purpose. "You scared the shit out of me. What are you doing here?"

Lightning cut an arc through the rain — too close — loud thunder right on its heels. "I was walking. You passed me on the road."

After snugging the boat down, Sarah climbed inside the F-150 and pulled the trailer out of the water. Together they strapped the craft down tight against the rollers and hopped into the Ford. Thunder pursued the lightning relentlessly, each flash and boom producing an involuntary flinch. The rain had settled into a hard downpour, pounding the roof of the truck, sloshing the windows.

Sarah muttered, "I barely got out there before it came down in buckets. A drizzle I can stand." Her hair hung in thick curly ropes, and her eyes looked huge under dripping lashes.

"I wanted to go with you."

"I wanted to be alone." Sarah ground the starter, apparently forgetting that the engine was running, the sound drowned out by the storm. "Goddamn it."

They drove home without talking, peering intently through the windshield, the road a wet blur. The wipers frantically thumped back and forth, unable to keep up with the pouring rain. Fran's heart flip-flopped when Sarah slammed on the brakes, almost missing the poorly marked driveway. She recognized the mailbox, the familiar turns. Water had made a lake of the backyard.

Running toward the house, they brushed together through the back door. Fran didn't realize until they were inside how noisy it was outside. They leaned against the kitchen counters and looked at each other. She heard the clock and refrigerator and the muffled sound of rain on the roof. Now what did they do with this day?

5

Turning on lights, she closed only the southwest windows, knowing she and Sarah would be too hot if she shut them all. Sarah went upstairs and changed into dry clothes. Fran did the same and came out to find Sarah slumped on the couch, paging listlessly through a magazine.

Sitting on a chair, Fran asked, "Want to talk?"

Sarah looked at her over the top of her reading glasses, her dark eyes opaque, and grunted, "What about?"

"Whatever." She couldn't stand the silence anymore.

Sarah's mother had died at the end of January, and in April Sarah had turned forty-six. Do people finally grow up when their parents die? Or do they grab for life? Fran didn't know. Her own mother was mentally growing younger by the day.

Getting up, Sarah walked to the front windows. "I want to go away. I feel trapped."

Pain shot through Fran. "By me?"

"By everything." Rain slid down the glass.

"Your job?" The hurt subsided to a pulsing ache. It goaded her into movement. She got up and looked out the window with Sarah at sodden woods, drowned grass. Gray, gray, gray.

"I've taken a leave of absence."

Sarah hadn't told her. Feeling betrayed, Fran asked, "When are you going?" She'd forgotten this kind of hurt, as if someone were stomping on her heart, twisting her intestines.

"Today." Sarah's skin was pale under her tan, her eyes unreadable. "I'm sorry."

Struggling to keep from crying, Fran managed a grim smile. "Me too. Will you keep in touch?" She

6

didn't have the heart to rant and rave. Deep down she knew the hopelessness of keeping Sarah when she didn't want to be kept. She saw the desperation in her face, recognized how much she wanted to be out of here.

When Sarah was gone, having packed and left in less than an hour, Fran thought she'd die wandering the dreary house, contained by the weather. Taking an old poncho out of the closet, she walked through the drenching storm, half hoping she'd be struck by lightning.

The next day, Sunday, Fran visited her mother at Meadow Manor. The assisted-living home was located on the edge of town. The residents were forever escaping and roaming the surrounding fields, looking for something lost. Their minds maybe. Her mother had a bath of her own and a room with a view, in which were crammed her most treasured possessions — those few chosen out of a lifetime of collecting. They'd had to sell her house, Fran's childhood home. The next step would be a nursing home, but by then she wouldn't know who or where she was.

Her mother was sitting in the sunny living room among the other elderly residents, staring out the window. White hair crowned her head. From a distance it looked stylish. Small and fragile, she sat ramrod straight, her face infused by sunlight.

Fran's breath caught in a sob. "Hi, Mom. Nice day." The rain was gone. She couldn't help wondering if yesterday would have been different had the sun been shining.

Her mother frowned a little as if pondering who she was. "Where are the children?" She looked puzzled.

"What children, Mom?" Fran's two were grown and gone — her son to Florida, her daughter to Pennsylvania.

Her mother's voice dropped. "There were cats all over my room again last night. You'll have to talk to the staff. They don't believe me." It was going to be one of those days, when her mother lived on another plane, one inhabited by imaginary people and animals.

"Want to go for a ride?" Already Fran felt confined, the ache gnawing at her, making her restless.

Ignoring the helping hand, her mother stood.

Fran gave her a hug, a kiss on her soft cheek. How familiar her mother smelled, and for a moment she wanted to fall into her sweetness, travel back through the years, tell her how much she was hurting. She thought in her mother's affectionate response that she was momentarily the person she'd known most of her forty-five years, quick witted and discerning. She longed for one more intellectual discussion with her, when Fran would finally tell her how much she'd always admired her mind. Her mother had once accused Fran of forever thinking that she knew more than she did. The arrogance of children, Fran thought ruefully. Much of what she knew was rooted in what her mother had taught her.

It occurred to her that she could take her mother home to live with her now that Sarah was gone. But she'd be alone during most days. The house was relatively isolated.

The sunshine made them blink.

As she helped her mother into the truck, she wondered if she would be sitting in one of her kids' vehicles one sunny afternoon years from now, going for a Sunday ride. She assumed this kind of aging was hereditary.

"Here, let me help you with that." Reaching across her mother's lap, she unrolled the window a little. The hot air inside the cab rushed out. Yesterday's rain had cooled things off. "Where to?"

Her mother's blue eyes pierced hers. "Let's go home. You shouldn't leave the dog alone too long."

Sighing, Fran considered getting a dog again. It would be company, a distraction. She drove to the humane society on a whim, half looking for somewhere to go.

The place was bedlam — barking, howling dogs and screeching, meowing cats. They stood in the small waiting room, crushed in a crowd of expectant people. Glancing at her mother, she wondered if this was a mistake. Her mother was scowling, her hands pressed over her ears. A young woman in jeans and T-shirt asked if they wanted to see the animals.

"Please," her mother said, extending her hand. "I'm Rhea Stadler. This is my daughter, Frances Dvořák, like the composer." A moment of gracious, though misplaced, lucidity.

The girl smiled. "Jody's my name. I'll show you around."

The pandemonium increased in decibels. Dogs pressed snuffling noses and trembling, whining bodies against bars, barking when the onlookers moved on. Cats looked at them out of untrusting eyes, as if the people were somehow responsible for the cats' captivity. In the last pen of the first aisle were three

9

puppies: two black, one brown. Curly hairballs with tails curved over their backs, pink tongues poking out between tiny teeth. Each would slightly overflow a hand. The sign on the door read, COCKAPOOS, ELEVEN WEEKS, HOUSEBROKE.

Come on, she thought, stooping and poking fingers through the bars. Surely they weren't big enough to be house-trained; they looked no older than eleven days. Standing on their hind feet, they nipped her enthusiastically with their little incisors.

"Want to see 'em?" Jody asked. She opened the cage, allowing one black pup to escape. He ran from them while the other dogs turned their snouts upward and howled their envy. Not fair, they seemed to say. Jody picked the puppy up and handed him to her.

"What do you think, Mom?" Fran held the small, wriggling creature close, feeling the heat of its body, the rapid beating of its heart.

"I'll buy him for you," her mother said. "Every child should have a dog."

"Thanks, Mom." That was when she decided to take her mother home with her on a trial run. She could let the puppy in and out the door. Maybe it would give her purpose.

But buying the little dog was not so easy. She signed a paper that said she would have him neutered when he was old enough, that swore she had a backyard where he would be safe from speeding cars. Only then, after her mother insisted on plunking down thirty-five dollars, were they out the door with Fran feeling vaguely unsuited to bring up animals.

"You didn't have to do that, Mom, but it was sweet of you."

"Nonsense. Children don't have that kind of money."

"Children don't have driver's licenses either or own their own homes," she muttered, helping her mother into the Ranger truck and placing the squirming puppy on her lap. Grabbing a pair of cotton work gloves from behind the seat before getting in, she said, "Put these on, Mom. He'll chew your hands." Her skin was so fragile.

"I'm tough," her mother said. Then, "Ouch."

"Want to stay with me for a while, Mom?" She started toward Meadow Manor, thinking they should get some of her clothes and stuff together.

Her mother looked at her quizzically. "Where do you live, honey?"

One of these days her mother was going to ask her her name, she realized. "You've been at the house lots of times, Mom. The log house in the woods. Remember?"

The puppy, who was wrapped in an old towel, managed to escape her mother's grasp and tumbled to the floor. "Is your lady friend there?" Restrained by the seat belt, her mother leaned toward the pup that was chewing on her tennis shoe.

Pain left her breathless and surprised. It had been so physical. "No. She left."

Her mother stopped trying to reach the dog and looked at her — blue eyes so clear and bright that Fran thought her confusion was all an act. "I'm sorry, Franny."

"It's okay, Mom." She tried to sound blithe,

wondering, as she often had during her relatively short lesbian life, how much her mother knew.

"You must be lonesome, honey."

Fran held back tears. It was better toughing it out alone. Any sympathy would let losoe a howl of anguish.

At Meadow Manor she flipped through her mother's wardrobe, cringing at the brightly colored polyester outfits. If out of style, they were no doubt comfortable. That was her mother's main concern these days. But her mother had once been a fashionably dressed woman. Filling a suitcase, Fran checked it out with her mother before snapping it shut. She'd already talked to the person in charge.

"Ready, Mom?"

Her mother looked confused. "Where are we going, honey?"

"Home."

The next morning she went over things with her mother four or five times. "Just let the pup out every few hours. And be sure to turn off the coffee. For lunch there's sandwich meat and cheese in the fridge. You know how to work the TV and the radio. My work number is on the pad next to the living room phone." She carried a cellular phone with her.

They stood in the doorway. The pup braced himself, growling while tugging on the toe of her mother's slipper. Her mother's mouth twitched. "Have a good day, honey."

Reaching down, Fran freed the dog's teeth. "Stop

that," she said, afraid he'd pull her mother off her feet. "I'll call you, Mom."

She drove to the dock where Nina and one of the men were loading her Quick Service delivery truck. Her job paid well, probably better than any work she could have obtained utilizing her college education. She hadn't even mentioned her bachelor's degree on the application.

Swinging the backpack that served as a purse over her shoulder, she climbed the steps. "Don't overload me," she shouted with a grin.

"Wouldn't think of it, honey," Nina yelled in reply.

Pouring a cup of coffee, she sat on a bench across from Bob Dombrowski, who was staring glumly into the steaming blackness of his mug. "Something wrong, Bob?"

He stirred a little and raised tired, bloodshot eyes. "My wife left me Friday night, out of the blue."

"I'm sorry, Bob. I really am." She was too. Mimi, his wife, was a looker. And Fran knew firsthand how much it hurt to have someone you love walk out on you. "You didn't have any warning?"

He shook his head. "She said she wanted out. She loved me but wasn't *in* love with me, whatever that means." His tone turned sardonic in midsentence.

"Where'd she go?" She didn't know what else to say.

"Would you talk to her, Fran? You're good that way." His eyes pleaded with her.

"What would I say?"

"She's at her mother's." He stood up and pulled a scrap of paper out of his uniform pocket. "I'll give you the name and number. Maybe you could meet over a beer or something and ask her what would make her happy. I'll do anything. Tell her the kids miss her."

"Guys meet over beers, and *you* should ask her what you can do." But she knew she would talk to her. She liked him, and she was vulnerable to such a plea right now.

Nina sat down next to Bob, which meant Fran's truck was loaded. He turned and poured out his tale of woe to Nina, who listened intently with a gleam in her eye that looked like humor. Her hair was cut in a crew cut, her ears pierced in rows, her shoulders broad from lifting loads, her nails chewed.

Fran took a few hurried sips of coffee and left. Stepping up into the twelve-foot step-van, she momentarily panicked. She pictured the house burning down around her mother and the puppy right now. Guilt would stalk her the rest of her life. Maybe she shouldn't have brought her mother home.

Before shifting into gear, she punched in her home number. It rang three times. "Mom, how is everything?"

Her mother's voice was calm. "Well, first the pup ran off, and I fell down chasing him. When I got back, a man with a gun was in the house."

When her mother got to the man-with-a-gun part, Fran's mounting horror turned to amused surprise. "You want me to have a heart attack?"

"You worry too much. Butch and I are doing fine. I couldn't get him to run away if I tried."

"Butch, huh."

* * * * *

14

When she returned home that night, she found her mother in the kitchen feeding Butch. The pup yapped in alarm at her appearance. A pot of water was about to boil over on the stove. Fran turned down the burner. "Hush, you silly dog." With one eye on her, the puppy began wolfing his food. "What'd you do all day, Mom?"

"Took a couple walks with Butch. Cleaned a bit, started supper." Her mother broke spaghetti in half and let it fall into the boiling water. "What'd you do?"

"Delivered packages."

"You got a college degree to do that, honey?"

"It pays well, Mom. Want some help?"

"You can fix the garlic bread."

Her mother's cheeks were pink, her eyes bright. Where was the woman she'd picked up Sunday? She had moved her mother into Meadow Manor because she got lost and forgot to eat and couldn't remember to pay her bills. What had happened between today and yesterday?

Then her mother said, "I want Butch to sleep in my room. He'll keep those cats away. They must have followed me."

Her words were a sharp reminder, yet Fran felt relieved. She would have hated to think she had put her mother into Meadow Manor for no reason.

Her mother looked up at her from the disparity of several inches, her eyes large behind silver-rimmed glasses. Where once a spider web of wrinkles crisscrossed her soft skin, there now were gullies. Thick, ropy veins formed blue ridges on her thin-skinned hands.

Fran's heart twisted.

II

The boat rocked on the flow of waves pushing steadily shoreward on a cool wind. Sarah would have wished it warmer, but she was closer to Canada than Illinois. Northern Wisconsin was known for many things — lakes, forests, fishing, wild rivers — but not warmth. Hardy people lived here, although sometimes in the summer there were days when the sun took her breath away and she slept in sweat at night.

The effect of a lowering sky turned the lake gray and finally she was enveloped by clouds that dripped with unshed rain. That's how she felt inside too.

She'd anticipated the freedom — no job, no lover, no family, no ties. Instead, anxiety pursued her as if there were an important appointment she couldn't remember.

When the northern pike struck, she was unprepared and jerked too hard, snapping the line. "Damn." Reeling in, she plucked the minnow bucket from the water and hauled up the anchor. As she started the motor, the first drops fell. It seemed as if rain followed her this summer. The drops stung as the boat planed out. She headed toward shore.

Padding around the cottage on bare feet, she listened to the rainfall. It reminded her of that last day with Fran. With a gesture and a wince, she pushed away the image of Fran's face. "Don't look so hurt," she said, startled by her own voice.

She'd been here only a few days but was already living inside her head. Last night she'd gone to the Hoar & Hound for pizza and met three women who were vacationing on a nearby lake. The place had been a zoo because of the lousy weather, and they'd asked if they could share her table. She'd invited them here tonight for dinner. Two looked to be together, the third a good friend.

This was a resort she and Fran had frequented over the years. She was lucky there'd been a cabin cancellation. Going out on the porch, she stared at the fog-shrouded lake. Water dripped from the aspens and pines leading down to the twelve-hundred-acre lake. Nothing puny about this body of water.

As she watched, the rain turned to a drizzle then ceased. The sun poked rays through separating clouds, turning the water blue and green, spreading gold, making more steam. She rushed out the door and down to the strip of sandy beach. Stepping into the cool lake, she raised welcoming arms.

The guy down the beach lifted his in answer. His face split wide in a grin.

"Hey, isn't this great? The sun! Come on in." She held open the screen door, letting it slam behind the tall dark-haired woman. "I made some snacks, and I'm taking drink orders. We'll go down to the beach. Okay? It's too nice to be inside, don't you think?" Was her eagerness too apparent? Shut up, she told herself. She didn't want to look desperate.

Amelia, Candy, and Georgie. Candy and Georgie were lovers, she was sure.

On the beach they spread out along the lakefront, their chairs facing the sun-dazzled lake, worshiping. The sun on water made them squint.

She set the crackers and cheese on a plastic table and pulled her webbed chair close to the water's edge. The man next door was swimming a hundred feet out, back and forth in front of their stretch of beach. He waved in passing. She put a hand up in answer.

"How long are you staying here?" Amelia asked.

"I haven't decided yet." Her computer rested in its case in the cottage, a silent rebuke. She'd told herself she would write, yet she hadn't put the first words on the monitor. "How about you?" She was watching the swimmer, hoping he'd remain friendly from a distance.

"I've been here only a couple days. Georgie and Candy were crazy enough to invite me."

Georgie stretched short legs toward the water, dipping her toes. "These lakes are cold. Do you fish, Sarah?"

All three tanned faces turned toward her. She nodded. "A northern bit through my line today, a big one." She leaned back and sipped her drink. Already the ice cubes were melting.

Then she looked at Amelia and saw Fran — even though Fran's eyes were a bright blue contrast to her dark, curly hair and Amelia's were a smoky hazel. Plain as day Fran sat in the chair, grinning that cocksure, crooked smile that Sarah found so sexy. Maybe if Fran had grinned, instead of smiling so painfully, she wouldn't have left. Closing her eyes for a moment, she opened them and met Amelia's questioning gaze.

They swam before going upstairs and changing clothes. She'd fixed an easy supper — potato salad, pan-fried fish, cole slaw. Like going out for Friday night fish on Monday, she thought.

Sitting on the porch, they watched the lake become a chameleon to the setting sun. Cicadas chirred; a loon called, its voice rising to a crazy crescendo before fading; another answered in calmer tones. She set the table on the porch, put the food on it, poured the wine.

"Did you catch these fish?" Candy asked.

"Yep. Haven't been doing much else since I've been here. The weather hasn't been good."

"You brought your computer," Amelia said, her sharp features softened by the mellow light filtering through the screens.

She laughed abruptly. "I thought I'd write. It's gloomy here when the sun doesn't shine. All I've done is fish and read, read and fish. These are perch and bluegills."

"Where do you work?" Georgie asked.

"At the library. I write for relaxation." She flashed a smile. It always made her feel vulnerable, talking about her writing. "Let's eat."

Afterward she took them out in the boat, driving slowly along the shoreline. Otters swam near the inlet to a creek — following the leader, blowing air, diving, snuffling, occasionally munching on caught fish. Taking a tour on the water was always a nice way to end the day. The lakes hereabouts were too large to leisurely cruise all the way around their banks, unlike the small jewels of landlocked water nearer home, each maybe a hundred-plus acres.

Passing a small bay, she pointed at a great blue heron standing long legged and motionless in the shallows. Two loons with young kept a careful watch from a safe distance. One adult rose and flapped its wings, yodeling a warning.

Before the women left, they invited Sarah to come to their cabin the next afternoon. They didn't have a boat, but Georgie said there was a nice beach.

Alone inside the cottage listening to the night sounds, she felt empty, lonely. Turning off the overhead light, she sat on the porch. Stars hung from a black sky. The lake monotonously lapped against the shore. Loons called eerily. Remembering how Fran loved it here, she felt uneasy, unfaithful.

She went to bed then, burying herself in a good book.

* * * * *

The next morning the sun covered the lake with a golden sheen. Birds flashed through the trees, bits of color and song, proclaiming their territory. The smell of pines and lake sweetened the air.

She opened the computer case, plugged in the laptop, watched the monitor flicker to life, and wrote.

When
the impossible happened,
the doctor told me to call her back.
The words choked me silent.
I watched, helpless,
knowing she willed her death.

After
I phoned my sisters.
The younger cried out denial.
The older said, "Well."
No words filled the void.

She was our mother.

She stared at the monitor. "Why did you die so quickly, so easily, Mom?" Sarah carried on solitary conversations like this. "Fran's mother should have died first. She's beginning to vegetate."

Knowing her mother's answer, she saved the words, turned off the computer, and went down to the lake.

The boat was fastened to the dock among the resort-owned aluminum craft. Walking out on the pier, she felt the heat of the sun through her bare feet. The sandy lake-bottom rippled under water so clear it was transparent. She loaded her tackle into the bass boat.

"Going out?"

The voice was so unexpected that she jumped, then turned. He was outlined by the morning light, making his features hard to distinguish. Shading his eyes, he squinted in the sun's reflection. She recognized him. The guy from next door.

"Yeah."

"Want company?" He grinned, showing off white teeth.

Surprised, she said reluctantly, "Sure, if you like to fish."

"I do, I do." He turned tail and hurried off the dock toward his cottage.

Stepping into the boat, she arranged her gear while waiting. Leaning back behind the steering wheel, she mentally kicked herself. Had she wanted company she wouldn't have chosen a man she didn't know. Gloomily, she longed for the isolation she had dreaded last night.

When he returned, she drove the boat to her favorite fishing bay and tossed the anchor into the weeds. Baiting her hook with a minnow, he put a worm on his. Their reels sang a duet as they snaked out.

He'd introduced himself as Troy Buchanan. He told her he was a designer. "I take space and make it beautiful and utilitarian." He offered another white-toothed smile while shaking her hand. He looked like a Troy — dark with curly hair, lovely brown eyes, wide shoulders tapering to slender hips, skinny legs. How unfair to straight womanhood that so many gay men were gorgeous.

An hour later she was glad he was with her. They'd caught twelve rock bass and three northerns that they'd tossed back and were now engaged in a fishing contest. Whoever snagged the most fish would enjoy a pasta dinner prepared by the other.

"You got a honey?" he asked.

"What?"

"I'm a recovering lover."

She laughed, dazed by the sun and a hot wind. It was wonderful to be out here today, frying already singed skin. "Why does everything that feels and tastes so good have to be bad for you?"

"Like the sun?" he asked.

"And french fries and steak and hamburgers."

"And fucking."

She howled. "Well, just indiscriminate fucking."

"Tell me about your girlfriend," he said.

"How do you know it's a girlfriend? Why couldn't she be a he?"

"For the same reason mine is a boyfriend, or was a boyfriend."

She pictured Fran, said her name under her breath. "She's cute, has dark curly hair like yours, blue eyes, fair skin, drives a delivery truck."

"Butch baby?"

"Naw. She has a college degree, and she's about my size." Two unrelated bits of knowledge.

"Toe-lockers." He grinned briefly out of a crimson face.

She wondered about her own skin. Better put on more lotion and a hat. "Want some?" She offered the sunblock. "What do you mean by toe-lockers?"

"That's when you're the same height and can touch toes and knees and chests and lips all at once. It's great. Makes me horny to think about it." His smile disarmed her. "Do I look as broiled as I feel?"

"Probably more so."

Carefully smearing her scorched body with lotion later that afternoon, she dressed in a T-shirt and shorts. Her shoulders were sore to the touch, her face sun stiffened, her legs too tender to encase in jeans.

Getting into the truck, she drove the few miles to the other lake. She could have taken the boat, but she didn't want to navigate the narrow channel between lakes after dark, although she had no plans to stay that long.

Amelia was waiting for her in the cabin. "You're fried."

"I know. I do it every year. I need someone to remind me to get under cover."

"Let's stay up here for a while. You've had enough sun."

They were standing in the small screened-in porch. "Sure. We can talk."

Opening two lawn chairs, Amelia gestured toward one. "Tell me about your writing."

It was the last thing she wanted to discuss. "You tell me about you. You said you sell real estate?"

"Yep. Do you own a house?"

Sarah shook her head. Fran owned the house. Good thing, looking at how things were now. "I've heard real estate is a dog-eat-dog world."

Amelia smiled. "I love it. I'm my own boss." She turned her dark face inquiringly. "Do you usually vacation alone?"

There was such a thing as being too tanned,

Sarah realized. Close up, Amelia's skin resembled leather. One of the best things about Fran was her skin, smooth and soft and fair. "I'm running away from my job, from my lover. And you, why are you here by yourself?"

"I work long hours. My last lover went off with a friend." Amelia looked lost for a moment. "There should be a law against that. It hurts."

"Yes." Looking through the screen, she could see Georgie and Candy, arms raised, tiptoeing into the water as if it was very cold. Their voices came to her on a warm breeze. Suddenly she was exhausted.

"Are you all right?" Amelia asked.

"The sun did a number on me. I could fall asleep."

"Want to lie down?"

All at once she felt terrible. "Maybe I should go home."

"I'll come with you. Make sure you get there." Amelia stood up. "Let me run down and tell Candy and Georgie."

Waiting in her truck, feeling worse by the moment, she saw the other two women climb the steps to murmur condolences.

"Got to watch that sun."

"I know." She was dizzy now, worried about the drive home.

"Come back tomorrow."

Falling into sleep with Amelia beside her, she remembered Fran the first time — flushed with expectation, the pulse in her throat gone wild.

"Sorry," she murmured. Was it so easy now? She'd chased Fran until she thought she'd just plain worn her down.

"Don't be." Amelia smoothed her hair back, her hand cool against her skin.

Hours later, she awoke in the fading light and saw Amelia sprawled in sleep — her mouth slightly open, her arms and legs spread defenselessly. She turned away, toward the soft lake breeze, and was pulled back into a stupor.

She dreamed Fran was caressing her, an open palm sliding over her breasts, her ribs. The hand slipped beneath her undershirt, lingered over her nipples. It moved down her body, stroking her belly, her thighs, traveled up the inside leg of her shorts. It covered her crotch. Fingers reached under the elastic and pushed inside. Her hips moved in automatic response. The fingers began a delicate circling dance.

She formed the words *Forgive me.*

Sunlight pierced her eyelids. Insistent birdsong made its way into her consciousness. She opened her eyes and found herself alone. Remembering the one-sided lovemaking, she touched her wet, delicate folds, curious to know how it had felt. She did the same with her breasts.

Feeling drugged and headachy, she forced herself upright and shuffled to the bathroom. Her face looked back at her, eyes swollen, skin puffy and red. Disgusted, she sat on the toilet with a grunt. Now she'd have to guard herself against further burning.

* * * * *

Troy was stretched on a lawn chair in the sand, wearing a cap, lightweight cotton slacks, and a T-shirt covered by a long-sleeve shirt flapping in the breeze.

She laughed. "We did a number on ourselves."

"Mmm," he murmured, his eyes hidden behind reflecting sun-lenses. "Going fishing?"

"Why not? I can't sunbathe."

She turned instinctively at the shadow overhead. An immature bald eagle stooped feet first no more than a hundred feet out and flapped heavily skyward carrying a wriggling fish in its talons.

"Did you see that? Did you see it?" she shouted.

"What? What?" Troy said, sitting up.

Hearing the water rippling against the shore, smelling the pines on the hill, feeling the hot sun toasting her head and shoulders, she experienced a moment of intense joy.

III

In a glaze of sweat Fran attempted to explain herself to Mimi over the phone. She felt like a fool. "Want to meet somewhere and talk?"

"I remember you now. You're a driver too." Mimi's voice was low, pleasant.

It vibrated somewhere in Fran's spine. "Seven years now."

"If you're going to throw in a plug for Bob, it's too late."

"I can tell him I tried anyway. He says he'd do anything if it would make you come back."

Mimi laughed softly. "Want to meet at Mary's Restaurant for ice cream?"

Her crotch tingled. "When?"

"Why not now?"

Fran lived thirty miles out of town with her mother and the puppy. Could she leave them and go off and eat ice cream? Of course she could, but she would feel bad about it. "How about after work tomorrow for a half-hour or so?" She felt uneasy being gone any more than necessary. That too would probably pass.

"All right."

The next morning she went to work with less trepidation. Butch rushed out the door with her, and she picked him up and handed him to her mother. "Take care of each other." The fresh, sweet summer morning filled her nostrils with woodsy smells. Blue jays screeched as they flew among the red pines, pursued by their muttering young. She jumped into her truck. "I'll call you, Mom."

At work Bob crouched over his coffee as if the world had stopped for him. He looked at her expectantly. "Did you talk to Mimi?"

"We're going to get together. Don't ask where or when. Okay?"

His face broke into a grin, and she warned him not to hope for too much. Nina came in and sat with them. Her truck was ready.

Fran climbed into the van and studied the stops on her route. She wondered briefly where Sarah was at this moment. Sarah loved summer mornings when the birds sang loudest and the dusty heat was still dampened.

Mimi wasn't at Mary's when she arrived. She called her mother while waiting in her truck.

"Is that you, Franny?" Her mother sounded annoyed.

Rush-hour traffic filled her ears. "Yes. What's wrong?"

"I'm fixing a casserole." The pup barked in the background.

"I'll let you get on with it then. I'll be home in about an hour."

"You told me that, honey. Butch is making a puddle on the floor." Fran banged the receiver as Mimi's blue Chevy Blazer drove into the parking lot.

She met her at the door of the restaurant.

"How you doing?" Mimi was tall and slender with high, flushed cheekbones, shining brown eyes, and thick chestnut hair that cascaded down her neck. No wonder Bob was stricken by her leaving.

The sight of Mimi made her want to run to the bathroom and check herself out in the mirror. Before leaving work, she'd brushed her hair into a semblance of order, splashed water on her sunburned face, studied the blue eyes so like her mother's. She didn't look bad, unless she'd missed something. With a smile she asked, "Want to grab a table?"

They ordered coffee from a dark corner.

Mimi said, "I haven't seen you since that dreadful banquet."

"Why was it dreadful?" She recalled having a good time.

Mimi laced her coffee with cream and sugar. "Bob drank too much, remember?"

She did. "I thought he was funny." Leaning on her elbows, she gazed into Mimi's tan face.

"You didn't have to go home with him."

"No." She didn't want to go home with any man, drunk or sober, but she couldn't tell Mimi that. "He asked me to talk you into going back." Then she realized how presumptuous she'd been to agree to do this. She hardly knew Mimi, or Bob for that matter. "I was feeling for him, I guess that's why I agreed to talk to you. Projecting or empathizing or something like that."

Mimi stretched her full mouth into a wry smile. "Someone leave you recently?"

Fran nodded and looked down at her coffee. A vision of Sarah fishing came to mind — her honey-blonde head intently bent over a hook on which she was impaling a minnow. Fran nearly cried.

"Then you're not living with anyone at the moment?"

Looking at Mimi through a haze of painful thoughts, she said, "My mother just moved in with me, and I bought a puppy the same day." She glanced at her watch. She'd have to leave soon.

Mimi gazed at her out of chocolate-brown depths. "Tell Bob that leaving was too hard to risk coming back."

Nodding again, Fran pushed back her chair, wanting to go before she shed any tears.

* * * * *

"She says she's not coming back," she told Bob at work the next day.

He moaned into the black liquid between his hands. "I hate being alone."

"Me too."

Showing brief interest, he lifted his head. "You looking for a man?"

Nina joined them. "No, she's not."

"How do you know?" he asked.

Nina winked at her. "Not every woman wants a man."

"What does she want then?" He scowled fiercely. "Not my Mimi."

"Guess my truck's ready." It was time to leave.

Thoughts tumbled around her head as she shifted gears. Her mother paid eighteen hundred a month to live at Meadow Manor. If only someone could tell her when her mother's grasp of reality, tenuous at best, would slip away completely, she could make a decision. But finding an assisted-living place with availability wasn't always possible. It was risky to give up the one they had.

At Kelso Mills Mimi stood in the reception room, her face a study in surprise. "Whew, I couldn't move when I saw the truck out there. I thought you were going to be Bob."

If Fran hadn't been astonished, she would have laughed. "This is my route. How come I've never seen you here?"

"I'm filling in for the receptionist today. Otherwise, I'd be upstairs out of sight." Mimi accepted the package and signed the delivery sheet. Her fingernails were painted rose.

Could she be a closet case? Not likely.

"Would you like to go to the movies? Or to dinner? I need to get out." Mimi's lips curved into a sweet smile, dimples denting her cheeks.

Fran felt fleeting shame. Here she was wondering how this straight woman's mouth would taste. But sexually Sarah had left her weeks ago. Fran was human and horny. Sarah was probably bedding down with someone else anyway. Maybe at this very moment. She frowned. It wasn't something she wanted to think about. "Yes to either or both."

"How about Friday night?"

At home that night Fran's mother said quietly, "Did you tell Matt I'm here?"

Fran looked up from the chop suey she was devouring like a starved person. "No. Why don't you call and tell him?" Matt, her brother, called their mother infrequently and saw her less. He had abandoned her care to Fran, who resented him for it.

"Somebody should."

"If he calls Meadow Manor, they'll let him know." The puppy lay under the table, munching on Fran's shoe. "Cut that out, Butch." She tried to shake him off, but he growled playfully, his little body whipping back and forth.

"Matt's a busy man."

"Too busy to call his own mother?" Fran said and was immediately ashamed.

"He's got a wife and children to look after." Her mother cooed at the dog, "Itsy-bitsy Butchie, don't chew on the footsie."

Butch gnawed more determinedly.

"Yes, he's got a wife, but his kids are grown, just like mine," Fran said sharply, unable to endure her mother's excuses for her brother's neglect.

"Chelsey called. She and Jamie are going to Florida to visit Jay."

Fran's heart turned over. Why was Chelsey going to visit her brother instead of coming home? It had been months since she'd seen her daughter. "What else did she have to say?"

"Jamie Lynn is her lover, isn't she?" Her mother looked as if she'd just gotten hold of a juicy piece of gossip.

"She didn't say that," Fran said, staring at her mother. "Did she?" She'd wondered about it herself, but she was amazed that her mother suspected such a thing.

"Honey, I met Jamie Lynn. They gave it away, just like you and Sarah did every time you looked at each other."

There was the pain, jabbing Fran in the heart, taking her breath away. She flushed. "Oh."

"They say it's hereditary. You must have gotten it from your father's side of the family."

She almost laughed, nearly challenging her mother's conviction that it couldn't have come from her side of the family. "I'll call Chelsey later."

Mimi was waiting on the front steps of her parents' house Friday night when Fran turned into the driveway.

"I need to find an apartment quick. You can't imagine how it feels to move back in with the folks,

34

especially when they're so disapproving," Mimi said as Fran backed into the street. "Or maybe you can."

Fran smiled grimly. "It's probably different living with my mother." It was hard to tell who was the caretaker.

Mimi stared out the window, her voice suddenly flat. "Do you have kids?"

Perhaps that's why Mimi wanted to go out, to talk to someone who had been in her shoes. "A son and a daughter — both grown, thank god."

"Mine too. I had them young. They're still living at home, though. Where are yours?"

She told her.

"I have a million questions. Do you mind?"

Fran remembered the need to talk when her husband, Karl, had left. "Shoot."

"I feel so guilty."

"Mmm." She nodded. "I guess everybody does." Even when he's the one who walks. She had been relieved when Karl decided to move out before she did. She thought the kids would blame him instead of her. Yet she'd wondered why she wasn't good enough for him, why he'd fallen in love with someone else.

Mimi looked out the windshield. "I thought If I stayed any longer I'd never get out."

She agreed. "There comes a time."

Mimi turned her head toward her side window and talked as if she hadn't heard. "There's no good time to leave. You're a shit if you do."

"It takes guts to pack up and move out when no one wants you to." She was trying to make Mimi feel better, but Mimi threw her a watery-eyed glance. Hey, she wanted to say, this evening's supposed to be fun.

"Where are we going?" Mimi asked.

"It's such a nice night, I thought we'd get carry-out and go to Lakeside Park."

They sat in the bed of the truck down by the marina and ate subs and chips. There were no empty picnic tables or benches. People were launching boats and taking them out; others were on the water in sailboats, speedboats, sailboards, and Jet Skis; and the rest of the crowd was watching — like them.

"How old were your kids when you got divorced?" Mimi asked, her eyes on the lake.

A breeze carried the smell of weeds and fish. If it was possible, Fran would bottle evenings like this to uncap during the winter months. "The youngest was sixteen, a junior in high school." Seven years ago, yet it seemed like an entire life had been compressed into that short time span. "How old are yours?"

"Nineteen and twenty-one. They're madder than hell, or maybe they're hurt."

"Mine weren't happy." She'd been surprised when they'd held her as responsible as Karl. Her son, Jay, had been briefly furious with her. Chelsey's anger had been longer lasting and more subtle. They had stayed with her, though, because Karl had moved in with his new love.

"This was a good idea. It would be nice to have a boat for nights like this."

Fran was never prepared for the pain. She and Sarah would have been on the lake in Sarah's boat tonight had Sarah not left. "Did you really just up and walk out?" Fran asked, momentarily glad that Mimi wasn't gay. She didn't need any more baggage. She felt that she was dragging a ton of it around with her.

"We had a fight over the kids. Their girlfriends practically lived with us, eating and sleeping over. I was cooking for six people and cleaning up after them. I'd had it. And then I realized I'd had it altogether and wanted out." Mimi paused for a bite of her tuna sub. "I don't know how many times I told Bob if he slapped me again that would be it. So I left."

"Bob hit you?" She stared at Mimi.

"Not for the first time. Your husband never knocked you around?"

Fran shook her head.

Since Sarah had left, Fran scanned the yard for her truck and boat whenever she returned home. It was stupid to let herself in for the disappointment, but an irrational hope always seized her about a mile away. The house was dark and silent and she glanced at the VCR clock after letting herself in. It was only eleven. Climbing the stairs, she pressed an ear to her mother's door and heard a soft woof. She quietly footed it along the balcony to her room.

Turning on the bedroom light, she emptied her pockets onto the ancient dresser. She'd been in an antique-buying phase when she bought the bedroom set. The furniture was large and dark. She stripped off her clothes and washed in the adjoining bathroom before flopping onto the bed. Leaning against the tall headboard, she picked up the book she was reading. She didn't open it, though; she was still thinking about the evening.

She'd dropped Mimi off at her parents' house

around ten-thirty. Mimi had thanked her and asked if she wanted to go apartment hunting with her the next day. Fran couldn't but said when Mimi wanted to go out again, she should let her know. Mimi had said tomorrow night, Saturday, sounded soon enough. They'd go out for dinner.

She couldn't figure out if Mimi liked her especially or desperately wanted company. She hadn't planned to spend all her evenings with a straight woman. And if Mimi by some miracle was queer, she feared so much unresolved baggage. Mimi had these boys, men really, who wanted their mother back. And there was Bob, who would have her hide if he thought she had a carnal interest in his wife. It was enough to quench all desire.

How comfortable life had been when Sarah was here. She slid down under the sheet. A warm, piney breeze blew over her. As she shut her eyes, her hand stole between her legs.

IV

Sarah and Troy were casting for muskies under a black sky pulsing with stars. It was nearly ten-thirty. The shoreline loomed nearby, a mass of tangled shadows. Dark wavelets lapped the boat. Troy had assured her that this was the best time to catch muskies. They each wore a small miner's lamp attached to their forehead with an elastic strap.

Sarah's heart thudded with alarm. "It's spooky out here." She was afraid that if she caught a fish as large as a legal muskie, it would pull her into the water, and she knew they were casting into a huge weed bed. "I have weed phobia."

Troy laughed softly and gave his rod a sudden jerk. "Don't panic, cookie, but I've got something very big."

She reeled in her lure and grabbed the oversize net.

He grunted in his efforts to keep the line taut. The drag sang in the night, and the tip of his rod moved to and fro as it skimmed the water. The fish surfaced once maybe six feet from the boat and came down with a splash that got them both wet. Troy laughed again, wildly, nervously. When the fish was finally close enough for them to see, it dove.

"It's a giant, Troy. How are we going to get it in the boat?" she said. She thought her heart was going to jump out of her chest. She fished this bay every day, but the darkness disoriented her. Even the docks looked dangerous.

"We're not. It's best to keep them in the water if you're going to release them. I'll just get the lure out of its mouth while you net him against the side of the boat."

As the muskie flopped in the net, Troy measured the fish at close to forty-five inches. He took a pair of mouth openers and stuck them in the huge mouth, then took needle-nose pliers to remove the lure.

But the lure wouldn't come out. The muskie fought to get away, splashing them. She struggled to hold the net against its weight.

"Fuck," Troy said as the fish splattered them again. "Every time it does that, the hooks go deeper."

"Reach in the gills. See the lure. I'll pull it out once you've got it loose."

Flicking its tail in their faces, the muskie disappeared into the depths. Troy's grin was illuminated by the miner's light.

"Thanks for the help," he said. "Now it's your turn."

She frowned and shook her head, wondering again if she wanted to hook such a monster fish.

He reached out and gave her a friendly slap on the arm. "Hey, it's a big thrill. Nothing like it. It's better than sex."

"If you caught a muskie every day, it wouldn't be." Picking up her rod, she cast into the black lake. It was eerie, hearing the plunk of the large lure as it vanished into the darkness.

When a fish struck her bait and ran with it, it was like hooking a boat moving in the opposite direction. At first, she couldn't speak as she fought to keep the slack out of her line.

Troy said, "Hang in there, cookie. It's just a matter of tiring it out.

By the time she brought the muskie aside the boat so that Troy could net it, her arms were leaden.

Troy measured the muskie. "Thirty-seven inches, cookie. You got yourself a keeper. It's your first. You're entitled."

"No. Let's release it and call it a night." She didn't want a fish that big in the boat.

"Sure you want to quit?"

"This isn't my kind of fishing, Troy. I like to read at night and fish during the day."

"Let's go to my place and have a drink."

"First I'll put my gear away," she said as he snugged the boat up to the pier.

His cabin looked just like hers. The clock over the

fridge pointed to eleven forty-five. "I'm not a night person," she remarked as he poured vodka into two glasses.

"But it was exciting, wasn't it?" He stretched out in a chair on the porch and raised his glass. "To fishing."

She choked on the liquor. "Water it down a little, Troy, will you?"

"A health drink." He poured more juice into her glass, then asked, "Are you looking for a roommate?"

"I suppose I will be." He came from the Fox Valley too and would be going home on Saturday.

He stretched his arms wide, offering himself. "I'm clean and orderly and pay my bills on time. Will I do?"

His lover was gone, as was hers. Why not? "Okay. Do I have to sign a lease?"

"No, I own the place. Just pay me some rent and half the utilities. I need help."

She smiled. "All right."

"I was afraid you might move in with that woman who spent the night there. I saw her leave early in the morning." He wagged a finger at her.

She laughed, embarrassed. "Hey, I was so out of it, I didn't know she was there." And now what was she going to do about it?

"Are you going to see her again?"

"I don't know." Could she pretend she remembered nothing? For all she knew it had been a dream. She finished her drink and he walked her to her cottage.

* * * * *

Amelia toed the sand outside Sarah's cabin the next afternoon. "Just wondering how you were. Is the sunburn better?"

Sarah sat on the porch steps, her chin in her hands. "I'm okay. Thanks for making sure I got home the other night." Had it only been night before last?

"What are you doing with yourself?" Amelia looked uncomfortable.

"Reading, fishing. We're going out in the boat this afternoon. Would you like to come?" she asked.

"Who's we?" Amelia asked, frowning a little.

"My friend Troy and me." She told about their muskie fishing last night. She'd slept in today; that was why they were so late getting out.

"I'd love to. I have my gear with me. We haven't done any fishing." She gestured at the Taurus wagon parked next to Sarah's truck.

"Good." Sarah hopped to her feet and went inside to get her rods, tackle box, and bait.

Troy was sitting in the bass boat, arms crossed, feet up, cap pulled down over his eyes. He got out when he saw Amelia. "Another fisherwoman? Great." While Amelia stepped into the front of the boat, he asked Sarah with gestures and grimaces if she wanted him to beat it.

"Of course not. Get in," she said, wanting to laugh aloud at his antics.

They sped to the bay where they had fished for muskies last night. It looked friendly in the partly cloudy day. She turned off the Evinrude, and Troy leaned over and let the anchor fall through the weeds to the bottom.

A threesome was safe. Casting her favorite lure, a glaring orange Mepps, she felt the familiar calm settling over her. Every problem seemed solvable when she was in the boat with her rod in hand. She didn't want another woman so soon, did she? She'd had plenty of women before Fran. It was Fran who lacked experience in that department. Sarah had been her first.

After casting without success, she baited the hook on her other pole with a worm and tossed the line in. Watching the slip-bobber soothed her. Other than asking for the bait to be passed, no one had spoken more than a few words.

"First fish of the day." Troy grinned as he held up a large perch. "Want to keep it for dinner?"

Jerked out of her reverie, she said, "I thought we were going to eat pasta, not fish."

"You got a bite, Sarah," Amelia said.

Troy released the perch as she reeled in a northern so small that they teased her about it.

"You girls want to come over for supper?" Troy asked later, as they emptied the boat of fishing gear. "I'll understand if you want to be alone."

Without glancing at Amelia, she said quickly, "Sure, I never turn down a free meal."

"Neither do I," Amelia said, "but I better drive back quick and tell the others."

"How about a swim first," Troy said.

They walked into the lake until the water closed over their shoulders; then one by one they dove into the coolness of it and came up spouting, shaking it from their hair.

When Amelia left that night, Sarah walked her to

her car. A loon called crazily from the lake, another answered. She thought of muskie fishing with Troy and shivered.

"You cold?" Amelia put an arm around her.

"No." She pulled away a little.

"Can we be friends, Sarah?"

"Sure." She patted Amelia on the back. "Sounds good."

It turned rainy toward the end of the month. Troy and Sarah fished in rainsuits. Amelia joined them, persistent as a fly. At the end of the last day, after casting for northerns on Lac du Flambeau, they loaded the boat onto the trailer.

Troy asked her if she wished to be alone with Amelia that night.

She said, "Sorry, but I don't want to be with anyone. Fran and I used to come here on vacation."

As if that explained everything, he nodded.

The next day she followed Troy home. Parking in front of a two-story red brick house with white shutters, she switched off the engine.

Troy proudly walked her through the large, sparsely furnished rooms. Light diffused by shade trees filtered into the many windows. The floors downstairs were oak, covered in part with oriental rugs. It was a formal house with an entryway, a living room, a dining room, a den with a half-bath, a kitchen, and an enclosed porch overlooking a ravine. Upstairs off the hallway were four bedrooms and a full bath. Those floors were carpeted.

"Very nice," she said, thinking of Fran's more casual log house with its open concept. It would be like comparing apples to oranges.

"Do you have any furniture to move?"

She did, of course, but she couldn't imagine telling Fran she was going to remove her things from the house. She'd have to get her clothes, though. "Well, yes, but —"

"Don't leave your stuff, cookie. That's always a mistake," he warned.

"It's different."

"You're thinking you might go back. Is that it?" He peered into her face, his dark eyes concerned.

"I might."

"Don't let too much time pass."

"I'll have to get my clothes. Soon."

They ate pizza on the porch that night. Troy filled the feeders, and the birds flocked to them. She thought she saw a fox in the trees at the edge of the yard.

"I've seen a whole family of them," he said. "Think you'll like it here?"

"I do already. I'll bet that ravine is filled with wildlife."

"Why did you leave Fran?" he asked.

She shrugged. "I don't know. I miss her."

"Maybe you should give it another try."

"Why did your lover walk?" She'd been wanting to ask.

"Dale was, is, his name. He was fooling around. I suggested he go."

46

* * * * *

She called the library the next day and told the head librarian she was ready to return to work in two days' time. That night she phoned Fran around six.

"This is Sarah, Sarah Nichols," she said, caught by surprise when an older woman answered.

"Do I know you?" the woman said.

"Rhea? Is that you?"

"Yes." A dog barked, and she said, "Hush, Butch."

"Fran's not there?"

"No. Do you want her to call you? What's your name again?"

"Sarah. I lived with Fran for years."

"Sarah, Sarah," the old lady said as if trying to place the name. Then her voice lit up with recognition. "Sarah. Of course. How are you, honey?"

"Okay."

"Franny misses you."

Hanging up, she wondered if Fran really did miss her and why she wasn't home and whether her mother had moved in.

As she put the finishing touches on dinner, she waited for Fran to call. Troy came home first. They ate. Around eight-thirty the phone rang.

"I'll get it, cookie." He pushed his chair back and went into the kitchen. They had been sitting on the porch, talking. "I've got to get my act in gear anyway and put my stuff from vacation away."

The call was for her. Her heart raced as she picked up the receiver. "Hello."

"Sarah?" Fran said. "Mom wrote your name and number by the phone."

"Your mom's living with you?"

"Yep."

"And you have a dog?"

"Yes. What can I do for you?"

She was being nosy. "Sorry. Just curious."

"How was your vacation?"

"Good." She started to talk about the fishing and then stopped.

"Congratulations. You always wanted to catch a muskie." Fran sounded cold. "You were up north?"

"Yes," she admitted, wishing she'd kept her mouth shut.

"Where'd you stay?"

"Where we used to go. They had a vacancy." She felt guilty.

"And you've got a place to stay in town?"

"With a friend, someone I met up north. Troy Buchanan. Do you know him?"

"No. Should I?"

"I thought you might," she said quickly. "He's one of us."

"So I suppose you want to collect your things."

"My clothes and personal belongings."

"This isn't a storage unit," Fran said.

"I know, Fran. But most of the furniture is ours, not mine." How to divide it? And where would she put it? There wasn't room here. "If I move into my own place, I may need some of the larger things. We can talk about it then."

There was a pause. "When do you want to come for your stuff?"

"How about tomorrow. Will you be home after five?"

"If I'm not, I'll tell Mom. She'll let you in, if she recognizes you. She's a little forgetful."

Be there, Sarah wanted to say, but she had no right.

V

The question was, did she want to see Sarah. Fran stood by the phone in the kitchen, watching her mother rinse off dishes, waiting for the nausea to subside. Damn. Just when she was getting used to Sarah being gone, she was back. So much had happened in three weeks that it seemed like months had passed.

Her mother glanced at her. "Was it what's-her-name?"

"Sarah, you mean." Fran began loading the dishwasher. "Look, Mom. I may not be home until late tomorrow. She's coming by to pick up her clothes. Is that okay with you?"

Her mother leaned against the counter and attempted to look into Fran's face. "You don't want to see her, do you?"

"I have to meet someone, but if I get away soon enough, I'll come home." She was trying hard to be casual.

"Look, honey, I know how you feel. Your father left me once when you were a baby. He didn't want the responsibility. It hurts."

Staring into her mother's blue eyes, she wondered if that had really happened or if her mother had made it up. "You never told me."

"There's a lot I haven't told you."

It made her question briefly what was locked away in her mother's mind, gone forever. Then Mimi called.

"I'm bored," Mimi said. Fran had helped move her into an apartment on Saturday, the second of September. "I never spent so many nights alone. I'm not good at it."

Fran was never without something to distract her — a book, a crossword puzzle. "Nothing on the tube?"

"Monday night football. I've watched enough sports to last me a lifetime. Want to come over?"

It was a good half-hour into town. Once she got home she usually stayed there. "Can't. Sorry."

"Oh, well, I guess I'll watch some trash. Are you still coming over for dinner tomorrow?"

"I'll bring the wine."

"Yeah, and an appetite. I'm used to cooking for hungry men."

" 'Night, Mimi."

Her mother's gaze was on her. "Is that woman after you?"

"Don't I wish." She grinned sheepishly. "What to play spite and malice?"

"I'll beat the pants off you." Her mother got the cards out of a drawer and pulled a chair up to the kitchen table. Whenever she moved, the dog jumped to grab her pantleg. He shook his head and growled fiercely, his feet sliding on the linoleum in a losing battle to stand his ground. "Stop that, Butchie. You'll ruin my favorite slacks." They were her black polyester, elastic-waist pair, the ones frayed at the hems.

"You never sound like you mean it, Mom. That's why he doesn't listen." Fran sat across the pine table from her mother.

"Who cares, honey? He's just a pup." Her mother shuffled the cards like a professional. She had once been a formidable bridge player. At Meadow Manor she'd garnered a foursome, but nobody could remember what was trump, much less what had been played. Now she dealt out their piles of twenty-six and two hands of five.

Fran picked up her cards and discarded a queen, wondering if this was to be her lot for the fore-seeable future. "Do you miss Meadow Manor? Is it lonely for you here?"

Her mother looked perplexed. "Don't distract me." She took her games seriously.

There were little things that disturbed Fran — like when her mother played cards off her discard pile instead of the pile she was supposed to be playing from. Yet she continued to win, beating Fran night after night.

The light dimmed and faded outside the open window. The night breeze was warm and nutty, smelling of fall. Fran counted her age in summers, and the onset of autumn meant another year had passed. Playing cards with her mother took her back to her childhood.

After she'd lost four out of five games, despite her mother's misplays, she called it quits. "That's enough. I'm going to eat at Mimi's tomorrow. So don't wait supper. And don't forget that Sarah will be coming."

The next night Fran met Mimi at her apartment as she was unlocking the door.

"How's Bob?" Mimi asked.

"All right, I guess." Funny how you made assumptions about people only to have them blown away, she thought. Now she looked at Bob and saw a strutting male, territorial and possessive, and found it difficult to be civil to him. "Why?"

"He keeps calling me." Mimi tossed her purse on the worn Danish modern couch she'd taken out of her parents' basement.

"How'd he get your number?" She set her backpack on the floor as she closed and locked the door.

"From my dad. He's on Bob's side." Mimi hung her coat in the closet.

"And your mother?" She walked to the patio door, which looked down on the parking lot. The apartment was on the second floor.

"She would never cross my dad. He'd have a shit-fit."

"Does he hit her?" She looked out the second-floor window at the parking lot.

"You're hung up on this hitting stuff, aren't you?"

Turning, she met Mimi's gaze. "It doesn't sit well with me."

Mimi shrugged, her face sharpened by weight loss. "You can push a man only so far. Sometimes you ask for it, you know."

Fran was appalled. "You've got to be kidding. No one has a right to slug anyone." Except their own kids, she thought wryly. There was always a glitch in everything.

Making a chopping motion with her right hand, Mimi said, "All right. I don't want to argue about it. I just asked about Bob, was all."

"Sorry. It's none of my business." It really wasn't her concern. Why would she want to get mixed up in it?

"It's okay. Want to uncork the wine and pour us a glass while I work on dinner?"

"Sure."

"I cooked up some homemade spaghetti sauce after I talked to you last night. We'll have garlic bread and a salad to go with it."

"Sounds good. My mother's been doing most of the cooking. It makes her feel useful. But she forgets essential ingredients — the eggs in the potato salad, the meat in the casserole. You never know what to expect when you take the first bite. She used to be a first-class cook."

"Poor thing," Mimi said.

She hadn't thought of her mother in those terms. It gave her pause. What was it like to forget even the most basic skills? "Butchie gets the leftovers. He's always thrilled."

Mimi laughed.

Handing Mimi a glass of wine, she asked, "Now what do you want me to do?"

"Sit. Talk to me."

Sarah's truck was parked behind the house when Fran arrived home around nine-thirty. Her mother was usually in bed by this time of night. Fran had left Mimi's early and under protest because she was worried about her mother being alone so long. She hadn't expected to find Sarah here.

She could see them at the kitchen table as she let herself in the back door. Her mother must have roped Sarah into a few games of spite and malice. They looked up at her — her mother expectantly, Sarah warily.

"Did you have a nice evening, honey?" her mother asked.

"Yes, Mom. Hello, Sarah." She stood inside the door, feeling awkward.

"I should go." Sarah looked at Fran's mother as if for permission.

"After we finish our game," Fran's mother said firmly.

Sarah raised her hands in a helpless gesture. "Your mother asked me to stay for dinner."

Fran wasn't surprised. Her mother had probably made enough for two people, forgetting that she wasn't coming home.

"Your turn, dear," her mother said to Sarah.

"I've won one game out of four." Sarah turned back to her cards and misplayed. "Look what I did! What a dope."

Fran smiled faintly at Sarah's nervousness leaking through. "She beats me all the time too. Did you find your clothes?"

"They're in my truck."

On her next turn Fran's mother played out her cards, winning handily. "There! I'm so sorry, dear. I hope you don't think badly of me. Another stroke of luck."

"You're out? Already? You'll have to give me another chance to win sometime."

"Anytime."

"Thanks for dinner, Rhea." Sarah got to her feet. "Will you walk out with me, Fran?"

"Sure. Come on, Butch. Time for your nightly tinkle."

Outside, the pup's ears and tail stiffened in alarm and he barked at the shadows.

"I didn't intend to stay," Sarah was saying. "She had the table set for two. Didn't you tell her you weren't coming home?"

"Of course I did. What did you have to eat?"

"A tuna casserole.

"How was it?"

"Honestly?" Sarah hesitated. "Something was missing."

"She and Dad belonged to a gourmet group at one time." Fran sighed.

Sarah opened the door of her truck. "It must be hard for you and for her."

Reverting to habit, she confided in Sarah. "I can't decide whether to keep her room at Meadow Manor or not. Maybe it's worth the expense just to hang on to it in case she has to go back suddenly."

"Afraid I can't advise you on that. I lost my crystal ball. Why don't you talk to your brother?"

She snorted. "Fat lot of good he is. He calls maybe twice a month. He almost never comes to see her."

Sarah climbed into her truck and unrolled the window. "Tell me when you're going out for an evening. I'll come over and spend time with her."

"It hurts to see you, Sarah."

"Me, too." Sarah waved out the window as she drove away.

Fran called for Butch and returned to the house. Wind rustled the leaves. If it hurt Sarah to see her for the same reason it pained her, because she still cared too much, why had Sarah gone somewhere else to live? She would never ask her for favors.

The night was dark, making it difficult for Sarah to see the blacktop. Periodically, she swerved onto the berm as if she were drunk. She'd had to bite her tongue to keep from asking where Fran had been. In the end, she'd been torn between the urge to run and wanting to stay. But if she stayed, she'd end up moving back in and she knew she'd feel trapped again.

It had been strange, finding Rhea there waiting

for her. She hadn't been able to say no to dinner or to cards after the dishes were cleaned up. Smiling to herself, she thought about the evening, the strange casserole that didn't taste quite right. Had some vital ingredient been missing? And cards. The old lady had beaten her soundly even though she had repeatedly played from the wrong pile.

She wondered which was more difficult, to have your mother drop dead when she was still mentally alert and in love with life or to watch her deteriorate by degrees. She had seen the puzzled look on Rhea's face at times as if she were struggling to remember something.

The house was lit up when she got home. The boyfriend Troy had thrown out was wanting to move back in. Dale had appeared on the doorstep shortly before she'd left tonight, surprised that she had become Troy's new roommate.

She slammed the truck door and grabbed an armful of clothes out of the truck bed, purposely making noise as she entered the side door by the garage.

"We're on the back porch," Troy called. "Come on out."

Poking her head through that door, she said hello. "I've got to carry my stuff upstairs."

"I'll help," Troy said.

"No, no, that's okay," she protested, seeing Dale huddled in a darkened corner.

"I insist. I'll be right back," he said to Dale.

He whispered when they met in her room. "Would you mind if he moved back in?" His face was pale. "I have to tell you, he's not well."

"Not well," she echoed.

"HIV positive."

"Oh." No wonder his face was white.

"Just until he tells his parents."

"It's okay, of course. You know, I can always —" she began.

He held up a hand. "No. You're not leaving."

She didn't know where she'd go anyway.

Sarah, who had a bachelor's degree in English composition and literature, worked at the information desk in the library — looking up data for the public, taking requests to hold a book or order one, finding misplaced material, showing patrons how to use the computers. Sometimes she would have several people on hold while others waited in person. But there were hours, especially during weekdays, when there was not much for her to do since she always had to be by the phone. Then she would read or talk to other staff.

The first day back at work she was in a daze over the new turns her life had taken. If she'd left Fran in order to be footloose, she was instead being bogged down with responsibilities. She wasn't altogether sure she wanted to be strapped in any way to a person who would need care. Selfish, yes. Troy's wit and capacity for fun had been the candle for her flame. Right now she wanted nothing more from anyone.

When she walked into Troy's home after work and heard the television, she went to the den to say hello. Dale, who was stretched out on the couch, looked at her morosely.

"Troy's almost never home before six," he said.

"Oh. Well, I'll go change and start supper."

"I'm not hungry." His nearly black eyes gave off no light.

"Look, Dale. I understand you didn't expect to find me living here."

"He didn't wait long to replace me," he said sullenly.

"I don't think he meant for me to take your place. I certainly don't intend to do so." She sounded stiff, her speech stilted. "He needed the money."

He gave a scoffing laugh. "Are you kidding? Honey, he's got money coming out of all his orifices."

"Maybe he didn't want to be alone," she said, wondering why she bothered defending him.

"If that's the case, it doesn't apply anymore."

She spoke without thinking. "Why do you dislike me? What have I done to you?"

He looked suddenly contrite, his eyes welling up and flowing over. He wiped them roughly with the backs of his hands. "I'm rude these days. Angry. I suppose he told you."

She nodded uncomfortably, wanting to flee. "Sorry," she murmured, afraid he would scream at her.

"So am I, sorry I lit into you. You look like perfect health incarnated. I'm afraid I hate you for it." He shrugged and smiled wanly. "I'll get used to you, though, and I'll eat whatever you fix."

"That's comforting," she said wryly.

When Troy came home, he found them in the kitchen — Sarah at the stove and Dale slumped at the table. Dale was drinking orange juice, but she had pulled the cork on a bottle of merlot.

"I needed a little balm to soothe me. Want some?" she asked Troy.

"It's my fault," Dale confessed. "I raged at her."

Troy poured himself a glass of wine and sniffed the air. "What's in the oven?"

"Enchiladas. I had a hankering for Mexican. So I picked up a few things."

"Gonna blow us to bits with all those beans," Dale said.

She looked at Troy and saw the pained smile. The skin under his eyes looked bruised. She had heard him in the hall and on the stairs last night. He had aged since yesterday.

"Did you talk to your parents today?" he asked Dale.

"I can't tell them, Troy. I want to stay here. I won't be any bother."

Troy loosened his tie. "I don't want to look at you. You understand? I'm probably next, because of you." His voice, low and controlled, resonated anger.

Sarah froze. She had no wish to witness this and started to leave the room.

"How long for these enchiladas?" Troy asked.

"Half an hour." She hesitated, then continued toward the stairs.

Troy followed. "Do you blame me?" he said on the steps.

"No." She'd be enraged too.

"I do," he said. "Guys are always taking care of their cheating lovers. I never understood that."

They were at the top of the steps, facing each other. His handsome face was troubled.

"You're right," he said. "I'm a shit."

"I never said that," she protested.

61

"I hate him." He gestured toward the stairs, his voice quiet and intense. "I was crazy about that guy. He put me through hell, and it's just begun."

She nodded, wanting to end this one-way conversation. "I understand, Troy."

He looked doubtful. "Okay. I'm going to change clothes. Will you be down to check on the enchiladas?"

Her appetite was gone. But she said, "Sure, yeah."

VI

After work the next day, Fran searched through the house, calling for her mother. Not an answering word or woof gave away her mother's or the dog's whereabouts until she headed upstairs. At the top of the open staircase was the balcony, off which were three bedrooms. Behind the two smaller bedrooms was attic space accessed through the closets.

She heard her mother's muffled voice raised in volume. "Here, honey, I'm here."

Butch rushed out of the closet in her mother's room. She bent to pat him.

Inside the attic her mother sat in a yellow pool of light going through picture albums. "Look, Franny, you have all the old pictures. Did you know that?"

"I stored them for you, Mom. Remember? When you moved into Meadow Manor."

"No, dear, I'm afraid I don't." Her mother looked up at her, her eyes a soft, muddled blue. "I didn't live here, did I?"

Fran's heart lurched. "No, Mom, you lived on Birches Lane, where I grew up."

Her mother frowned.

"In a one-and-a-half-story Cape Cod." Surely she hadn't forgotten.

"Silly of me. Of course, I remember." She laughed. Again she glanced at Fran with troubled eyes. "Where is my furniture?"

"What Matt and I couldn't use, I had to sell. Some things are still in the garage."

"I'd like to see them sometime," her mother said vaguely. She pointed at an old photo. "Look at these cute little kids."

Fran leaned over. "That's me and Matt."

"Your brother, Matt? How is he?"

"I don't know." Saddened though she was by the conversation, she couldn't hide her irritation at being reminded of her brother. He hadn't shouldered any of the responsibility for their mother.

"He's a busy man."

Knowing that her mother wanted to believe that, Fran fought back the urge to criticize Matt. Suddenly overwhelmed by grief, she said, "Want to go for a walk, Mom? It's nice outside."

"What a good idea."

Because it took her mother a half-hour to get

ready, by the time they stepped outside, they had maybe an hour of daylight left. Walking down the sandy driveway to the blacktop beyond, Fran noticed how the drying cornstalks in the field across the road shone in the September sunlight like a field of wheat in July.

Butch played tug-of-war with his leash, leaping and grappling with the leather that tangled around his short legs. He growled fiercely and dug his nails into the gravel berm, forcing Fran to drag him skittering along. She'd have to take him to dog obedience when he was old enough.

"Tell me when you want to turn back, Mom."

"About now, Franny. Let's sit on the deck instead."

But by the time they arrived home, it was cool on the deck with the sun slipping swiftly out of sight. So they went inside to eat the supper Fran's mother had made.

"Good chili, Mom," she said as it burned her throat. She coughed. "What did you use for seasonings?"

"You don't think it's too spicy?" her mother asked, gulping from her water glass.

"Maybe a little. Put some crackers in it." She got the saltines. "I've been thinking we probably should move closer to the valley." The trek to and from work every day took more than an hour out of her day. And she worried about her mother being so isolated. On top of that, she herself was lonesome.

Her mother looked up from her bowl with a puzzled expression. "Whatever you think, dear."

She'd have to put the log house on the market and, once it sold, take an apartment until she found another place closer to the valley. She couldn't afford to keep two residences.

Fran listed the house the next day, before she could give it further thought. She and Karl had built it together, working on weekends from dawn to dusk when the kids were little. First Karl had left, then the kids, followed by Sarah. The memories were like ghosts, haunting her.

From her cellular phone, she called Realty One. Since she knew no agents, she gave the listing to the woman on phone duty, an Amelia Rossiter, who arranged to meet her at the house after work the next night.

Fran had been arriving at work with only enough time to climb into her step-van and drive off. It was the only way to avoid meeting up with Bob, who now, instead of resembling a friendly bear, loomed large and menacing. Today he was standing on the loading platform with Nina.

"Shit," she muttered, getting out of her pickup.

"Where've you been lately? I want to talk to you," he hollered, jumping to the blacktop and striding toward her.

Glancing at her watch, she put one foot in her delivery truck and waited for him.

"How's my wife?" Bob said as he approached. His delivery van was parked next to hers, both backed up to the loading dock.

"Fine, I guess." She didn't know what else to say.

"She don't answer my calls anymore. She lets the answer machine talk, then never returns my messages." He looked hurt. "Tell her to call me, will you, Fran?"

"I'll tell her." She turned to grab the steering wheel and jumped when his fingers closed on her arm.

"You see her all the time, don't you?" His voice had dropped a register.

"No." She looked over his shoulder at Nina.

"Come on, Bob, the trucks are loaded. Time to go," Nina said, tugging on his sleeve.

He shrugged off Nina and let go of Fran. His voice was sullen. "She's my wife."

Fran pulled herself up, dropped into the seat, and turned the ignition. The engine drowned out her answer. "She's not a possession."

"What? What'd you say?" He had been turning away.

She put the step-van in gear and drove out of the parking lot. In her mirror, she saw him standing straddle legged, staring after her.

When she returned that afternoon and backed her truck up to the dock, Nina was waiting on the platform.

"You been here all day?" she asked, swinging out of the truck.

Nina jumped to the blacktop. "If I'm going to be running interference between you and Bob, I want to know what's going on."

"Nothing," she grunted. It was the truth. "Mimi needs a friend."

"That man's nothing to fool around with." Nina followed her inside while Fran inserted her card in the time clock.

"I don't want anything to do with him. He used

to knock her around." She went back outside. It was one of those mellow September days, where sunlight, burned out by summer's intensity, floated on a dusty haze.

Nina walked by her side. "All the more reason to not make him angry."

She stopped and faced her. "He thinks he owns her."

"Stay out of it," Nina warned.

Fran's gaze wandered to the rows of studs in Nina's ears, to the brush cut on her head. She'd never have the nerve to wear her hair that short. "That's what he wants, for her to have no friends."

"I suppose you're right. I wasn't thinking about her." Nina was chewing on her lower lip.

"Look, I appreciate your support, but I want to get out of here before he comes back."

"I'll do what I can."

Fran squeezed Nina's arm. "Thanks. It's good to have you on my side."

As she drove off, she saw Bob's van turn into the lot. Breathing relief, she was glad she wasn't seeing Mimi today or tomorrow. In fact, she had been trying to put some distance between the times they spent together. Not because of Bob, though, but because she was beginning to feel a little entangled.

Leaves were whipping around the yard in front of a wet wind when Fran parked in front of the garage Thursday afternoon. Thinking that someone else would rake them onto a tarp and drag them into the woods to decompose next spring saddened her, although she'd hated the job.

A tall, lean woman got out of a Ford Taurus and introduced herself as Amelia Rossiter. A white smile cut through the deep tan of her face. "I'd like to measure the outside and take pictures before the daylight goes."

"Feel free. I'll change clothes and be right back." She let herself into the house and called for her mother.

The house was empty. She knew it immediately, and the knowledge sent a cold rush through her as she ran up the stairs. Where could they be? Had they taken a walk? Although the skies threatened rain, even the wind was warm.

Hurrying to the end of the balcony, she went into her bedroom and tore off her work clothes, replacing them with jeans and a sweatshirt, then galloped down the stairs and into the kitchen. If her mother had left a note Fran figured it would be next to the phone, but there was nothing. She made a hurried, futile tour through the remainder of the house.

Outside, the Realtor had finished with her measurements and picture taking and was ready to start on the inside.

"I'm sorry," Fran said, "but I have to go look for my mother. She's wandered off or something." She held the door open. "Feel free to go ahead and do whatever you have to do inside."

The woman gave her an appraising look as if wondering whether she was telling the truth. "I'll help you look for her," she said. "I wouldn't feel comfortable inside alone."

"I'm just going to drive around a little and stop at a few houses. She would have a puppy with her." She described her mother and the dog and swallowed. Fear in the form of a heavy weight settled in her chest and made her frantic.

"I'll go in the other direction."

"Thanks. I'll meet you back here in an hour."

Fran turned into the driveway of a farm half a mile up the road from her place, spraying gravel from behind her tires and sending chickens squawking into the yard.

Knocking at the farmhouse door, she waited for someone to answer while staring at a John Deere tractor cutting alfalfa in the fields behind the barn. As she turned away, the door swung open an inch or two and a small child peered out at her.

"Mama," the little girl yelled. "Someone else is here."

Fran caught sight of the puppy behind the child. Butch wormed his way past her and out the door opening. The icy ball melted inside her, and she went weak in the legs. Picking up Butch, she held him close. He needed a bath.

A woman about her own age thrust the door open wide and invited her in. "I'll bet you're looking for your mother. We're having coffee in the kitchen." She lowered her voice. "My husband found her in the hayfield with the dog. She said they were walking to the store. I was going to bring her home soon."

Fran introduced herself, ashamed that she had never bothered to learn her neighbors' names, preferring that they remain anonymous.

On the way home she said, "Mom, you can't go off like that. You might have gotten lost."

Her mother sat slumped against the door, the puppy panting in her lap. "I just went visiting."

"Leave me a note next time. It scared me."

"I wanted someone to talk to."

She glanced at her mother. "At Meadow Manor you always had people to talk to."

"I'm tired."

"I'll bet you are." No telling how long she'd been wandering around before the farmer had come across her by the creek bank.

Rain began to fall, tiny drops spreading and flattening on the windshield. Her mother could have been caught in a downpour or, later in the season, a snowstorm. The thought crystallized her decision to sell the house.

The Realtor emerged from her Taurus with a huge umbrella, which she held over Fran's mother until they were inside.

"Let me fix you a cup of coffee or something," Fran offered as she turned on lights.

"No, thanks. I'll just measure and ask some questions. Then I'll put it all together for you."

While her mother stretched out in the den with the news on, Fran followed the woman from room to room, holding one end of the tape for her.

When they went upstairs to the balcony, the Realtor said, "Nice place. Who built it?"

"My ex-husband and I did. He was a builder; he *is* a builder."

"Is there a reason for selling?" The woman's eyes were the color of smoke, their depth lost in the caramel of her skin.

"My mother can't live way out here. The neighbors found her in a hayfield." But she could wander

71

away in the city too. Meadow Manor might be the only safe place. "And it's a long way to drive to work every day." She didn't tell her the other reason, that she was lonely here without Sarah, that the place had lost its allure.

They were standing in the doorway now, the overhead light casting a dreary glow over the foyer, barely reaching into the living room. Fran walked over to the davenport and switched on the goose-necked floor lamps. The room sprang to life.

"I'll be talking to you." Amelia smiled. "This shouldn't be hard to sell."

Then she was gone, and Fran went into the kitchen to start dinner. The puppy fell on her feet, and for the first time, she realized that he would cause problems. Few apartments took pets, and what would she do with him if her mother had to go back to Meadow Manor?

Depression gathered in the corners of her mind. She tried to sweep it away before it got the upper hand. With all the lights on, the kitchen still looked dark. Night had fallen and rain beat against the windows, forcing her to shut them. She remembered enjoying being closed in from the elements, but that was when Sarah was here and their relationship was the glue of her happiness.

It didn't work, she thought, tearing apart lettuce as yesterday's fried rice heated up in the microwave oven. You couldn't depend on someone else to make you happy. Yet people were social animals. They needed other people.

"Smells good, honey," her mother said, appearing in the doorway, looking refreshed. "Can I help?"

"Sure, Mom. You can set the table." Fran's spirits lifted a little. She thought of her mother, widowed nearly as many years as she'd been married. That was loneliness, not herself missing Sarah.

VII

Sarah saw the listing in the Sunday classifieds. There was a picture of the house with the price underneath it — $139,900 — followed by the specifications. Something akin to an electric current hummed through her when she recognized it as Fran's.

"Why would she do that?" she said.

"Do what?" Troy asked.

They were on the porch, sharing newspaper sections. Dale wasn't up yet. The leaves were beginning to turn, starting with the sumac, which burned crimson along the edge of the ravine.

"Fran's selling her house. She's having an open house today."

"Let me see," he said, looking over her shoulder. "Nice place."

"It's listed with Amelia. How about that for coincidence?"

"Does Amelia know who Fran is?" He settled back in his lawn chair, putting his feet up on another one.

"No." She felt betrayed. If she wanted to go back, she couldn't — not to the same house.

"You look unhappy," Troy said.

"I guess I am. I feel like she's making changes that permanently exclude me."

"Why don't you give her a call? You're on speaking terms, aren't you?"

She made a derogatory noise. "What right do I have to say anything?"

"Say what?" Dale said.

"Her ex is selling the house," Troy explained. "How would you feel if I sold this house?"

Dale lowered himself onto a chaise longue, set his cup of coffee on the cement floor, and reached for the travel section. "You wouldn't do that."

"Sure I would. I'd move into something smaller."

"There wouldn't be room for me." Dale glared at Troy.

"See? What you're feeling is normal, cookie."

"Why do you call her cookie?" Dale asked. "You used to call me cupcake."

"You're a cupcake, she's a cookie," Troy said with a shrug.

"I will call her." She went to kitchen and poured herself a cup of coffee, then punched in Fran's number. But when Fran answered, she hung up.

75

Troy came into the room and slipped an arm around her. "What do you want for breakfast? Pancakes, hash browns, eggs, hot cereal? You name it."

She got potatoes out of the bin and scrubbed them before putting them in the microwave. "The house was part of her marriage settlement."

"I wondered," Troy said. "It's kind of expensive for one person."

"I just don't want her to rush into this because I left. Maybe she can't afford it alone."

"Ask her."

"I can't."

Dale came in for coffee. "Why don't you ask me what I want for breakfast?" he said peevishly.

"Why are you such a pain in the ass?" Troy said.

"I want pancakes," Dale said, retreating to the porch.

"Me too," she said, trying to stay on Dale's good side.

"Quit pandering to him. He hasn't even called his parents," Troy said loudly.

"Why don't you call them and tell them their son is dying?" Dale yelled back.

"Christ, I hate this." Troy reached for the pancake mix. "All right, it's pancakes and American fries."

She didn't know what to make of their quarrels. "Did you always fight like this?"

"Does a bear shit in the woods?" Troy gave her a dark look. "No, seriously, we were once lovebirds, cooing over each other. Makes me want to puke to think of it."

"I wish you wouldn't do this in front of me. It makes me want to run." She was chopping onions to sauté with the potatoes.

"Sorry, cookie." He raised his voice. "Hear that, cupcake? Keep a lid on it."

"Me!" Dale sounded disbelieving. "You're the one who started it."

"Did I?"

"How do you know that I didn't contract HIV years ago, before I knew you?" Dale appeared in the kitchen. His hair stood on end, a dark frame for his pale face.

Troy stopped beating the pancake mix and looked at him. A funny expression crossed his face. "You cheated on me. I know that."

Dale disappeared onto the porch again. "There is such a thing as safe sex, you know."

"I didn't know you knew." Troy glanced at her again. "Okay, sweetie, no more, at least not today. Should we go to the open house? Amelia will be there. Fran won't, though."

"I'll think about it."

They parked on the road and walked in. The yard was cluttered with vehicles. Sarah looked for but did not see Fran's truck. It could be in the garage, of course.

Amelia stood in the foyer, dressed in a handsome gray suit, greeting people and handing out literature. She looked surprised to see them. "Hi, you two. House hunting?"

"Just looking," Sarah said. "Have you got any offers yet?"

"One already. This is a lovely home — secluded, yet with all the amenities." Amelia gave them a wide smile. "Stick around a while. I'll be leaving in less than an hour. Maybe we can go out for pizza."

Troy shot Sarah a questioning look.

"We could meet you at Antonio's at five-thirty. Would that give you enough time?" Sarah said, wanting to be out of here before Fran returned.

"Sounds good. Feel free to look around."

Troy stargazed at the beamed, cathedral ceiling. She stared at the stone fireplace, so clean that it looked like it had never been used, remembering the times she and Fran had done it on the rug in front of a hot fire.

"Let's go upstairs," he said.

Troy was nosing around Fran's bedroom and bathroom, looking in the medicine cabinet and closets. "You can tell a lot about a person this way."

"Why don't you just ask? I have inside knowledge."

He opened a drawer and pulled out a framed picture. "It's you."

Her vision blurred. "Come on. Let's go," she said.

Stuffing the picture back in the dresser, they left the room as another couple entered. "I've got to see the kitchen," he said.

Outside, the leaves crunched under their feet as they retraced their steps toward Troy's new Ford Explorer. When he'd picked it up yesterday, she'd realized that Dale had spoken the truth. Troy didn't need her rent to keep him afloat.

"You all right?" he asked, when they shut the car

doors behind them. The vehicle smelled like new leather.

"I'm fine." She watched for Fran's truck in the side mirror.

"Why did you leave her if you still care so much?" He sat with one arm flung over the back of her seat, looking at her.

"I only know I want to be out of here before she comes back."

Sarah helped Amelia shrug out of her coat in the booth at Antonio's. She and Troy had been drinking wine, waiting for her.

"It's a cabernet," Troy said. "Probably cheap, but not bad. Want some?"

"Please," Amelia said, then asked, "What brought you out today?"

"Curiosity, and we knew you were there," Troy said.

"The poor woman who owns that house has to sell because of her mother." She told them how they'd searched for Fran's mother.

"Sarah knows Fran," Troy said, then lifted an eyebrow and shrugged at Sarah's glare.

"Do you?" Amelia turned toward Sarah. "She seems very nice."

"She is." Sarah didn't get it. Why had Fran taken her mother out of assisted-living if she was going to be a problem? And why on earth had she bought a dog? "Where is she moving?"

"Closer to the valley."

"It is lonely out there. Her mother could disappear in the cornfields forever." She looked at Troy. "Do you think you should call Dale and tell him we're eating here?" They had gone to other open houses after Fran's and hadn't been home.

"He can fend for himself."

"He'll be mad," she pointed out, knowing his anger would be directed at her.

Fran had packed a couple chairs, a picnic lunch, and reading material in the Ranger around noon. Then she helped her mother into the front seat, put the puppy on her lap, and drove to the nearest lake with a county park. The day had started out sunny but was overcast by afternoon, yet the temperatures rose into the seventies.

Turned loose, Butch dashed around the sandy beach, barking at the waves. She threw his ball in the water, but he refused to more than wet his feet. No one had been in the park when they first arrived, but during the course of the afternoon several people showed up and Butch greeted them like long-lost friends.

"He'll never make a watchdog, Mom," she said after dragging him away from a dour-looking couple.

"Good thing. We had a dog that bit people once. You had to watch him every minute." Her mother frowned in concentration. "Did we come here when you were little?"

"I don't know. I suppose we could have."

They ate lunch and sat on the beach until four, when Fran packed everything up and loaded it back in the truck. By the time they reached home, the open house was over. Amelia had left an offer to purchase on the kitchen table with a note that she would call later.

Sinking into a chair, Fran read through the offer. The proposed buyers were willing to pay the full purchase price, contingent upon the sale of their house and an inspection. It would give her time to get used to the change.

"It's so quiet." Her mother brushed against her. "Is there a message from Matt?"

The machine was blinking from its corner of the counter. Fran pushed the button and listened to the tape rewind.

"It's me, Mimi. I'll be there about six tonight." The machine beeped and the tape stopped.

Fran glanced at the clock. "I'd better get dinner started."

It was dark when Mimi arrived. Fran hadn't seen her for a week and, when Mimi stepped into the light of the kitchen, she noticed the heavy makeup. She reached to touch her cheek.

"What happened?"

Mimi shrugged. "What usually happens when Bob loses his temper. It's okay. I asked for it."

"Let me guess. You said, 'Hit me.' "

"Where were you Friday night when he came over? I wanted to go to the movies, but you wanted to stay home."

"Why do you let him in?"

"He was threatening to break the door down."

"You need to get a restraining order."

They were standing inside the kitchen, their voices low and intense. She wished at these times that she hadn't become Mimi's friend. Part of her feared that Bob would follow his wife to her door. It frustrated her that Mimi took his abuse for granted. She felt as if she was in a catch-22, being Mimi's friend and Bob's coworker.

"Girls, girls, what's the matter?"

"Hi, Rhea. How're you doing?"

"Franny, don't argue with Sarah. Where are your manners?" Her mother's cheeks were bright pink, her eyes lively. "Come on in, Sarah. I'll take your coat."

A chill ran through Fran. "You mean Mimi, Mom."

"Who's Sarah?" Mimi asked.

"She used to be my roommate."

Her mother's eyes dimmed. "Sorry, I forget. A relationship's a relationship."

Now what was that supposed to mean? Fran wondered.

After dinner Mimi suggested they all go somewhere next Saturday. "You need to get out of the house, Rhea."

"I went for a walk and got into trouble. A trip to town would be nice."

When Amelia called, Fran excused herself and took it in the living room. "I'll sign the offer," she told her.

"Wait a couple days and see if any others come in. Often people need time to talk after an open house. You might get an offer without contingencies, or at least one that doesn't hinge on someone selling their house first."

"Were there many people here?"

"Yes. There was a lot of interest."

"I meant to ask you to start looking for something for me somewhere in the city. Something not quite so big, less expensive, but not your standard three-bedroom ranch either." She'd know what she wanted when she saw it.

"I'll send you listings as they come up. If you want me to look for you, you have to let me show you the houses you're interested in, because if someone else shows them to you, you have to buy through them."

"All right. I don't have time to look myself."

After cleaning up the dishes, the three of them played hearts. Fran's parents had taught her to play cards, had often played with her and her brother when they were growing up. Yet her mother had forgotten the cardinal rule, sometimes failing to follow suit.

Later, when she and Mimi stood outside in the cool night saying good-bye, Fran asked, "Can you see her slipping?"

"Some." Mimi squeezed Fran's hand and gave her a hug. "You never think about being a parent to your parents, do you? First you're the kid, then you're the mother to your kids, and later you're taking care of your folks, and I suppose even later you're the kid again. I hope I drop over dead before that happens."

"Me too," Fran said.

VIII

It wasn't dating if there were three of them, Sarah had told herself when they'd made plans to go to the late afternoon matinee and out to dinner. But now Dale was coming along, so it would seem like double-dating. Dale and Troy, she and Amelia. She didn't like it.

Amelia had made the suggestion over pizza Sunday evening, prefacing it with, "Are you doing anything next Saturday?" She and Troy, caught off guard, had answered honestly as they had a few minutes ago when Dale asked if he could go with them that afternoon.

"If you can go out, you can go back to work," Troy said as Dale climbed the stairs to get ready.

"I am. Next week. Although they'll fire me if they find out." He was a waiter.

"Just don't bleed on anyone's food," Troy called after him.

Sarah touched his arm. "Come on, Troy."

"When he gets sick, he's out of here."

"You don't mean it," she said, not quite sure.

He grinned at her wickedly, and she said what she was thinking.

"Why can't it just be you and me going out?"

"Don't I wish." He kicked the bottom step.

When Dale bounded down the stairs, looking darkly handsome, she could see clearly why Troy had once been crazy about him.

"I'm driving," Troy said. They were to pick Amelia up at her condominium.

They were early, so they bought their tickets and walked around the mall, window shopping. Sarah had forgotten what weekends at the mall were like there with wall-to-wall people.

"Let's try on some clothes," Dale suggested, standing outside Eddie Bauer.

"You do that," she said, plunking herself down on an empty bench seat. "I'll wait here."

"I'll stay with you." Amelia sat next to her.

Waves of people flowed past them, obscuring their view of Dale and Troy, who were going through racks of clothing inside the store.

"How was your week?" Amelia asked.

"Good, okay. Did you sell Fran's house?" She nearly choked on the question, but she'd wanted to call Amelia all week and ask. The bench divided the flow of people streaming past into two directions.

"We have an accepted offer. It's contingent on the buyers selling their house."

"So it might take a while," she said.

"The offer could run out before the conditions are met." Amelia shrugged as if tired of the conversation. "Could I see more of you, Sarah, and occasionally be alone with you?"

"I guess I'm just not ready to see anyone seriously."

"Do we have to be serious? What happened to just having fun?"

Maybe she hadn't given her much of a chance, but she thought Troy was more fun than Amelia. He and Dale were coming out of Eddie Bauer. They were laughing.

"Sure. I'd like that, but let's keep it light." She touched Amelia's hand and asked, "What's so funny, guys?"

Troy sobered immediately. "I'd forgotten what a flirt he was."

Dale grinned. "The clerk was so cute, I had to ask him if he'd like to go dancing."

They joined the directional flow heading toward the theaters.

"What'd he say?" Sarah asked.

"That he only dances with girls. What a squelch, and I could have sworn he was one of us."

"See? See?" Troy said. "This is what I had to put up with."

"Good thing we got our tickets ahead of time,"

Amelia remarked. The lines for the movies wound into the fast-food tables.

"Yep, we can go right on in." Troy led the way past the jostling, waiting people.

Toward the front of the line, Amelia paused to talk to someone in line.

Sarah, who was mindlessly following, nearly bumped into her. Seeing Fran threw her into confusion.

Fran gave her a small, knowing smile that made the flush starting at her toes speed upward. "Hello, Sarah. I didn't realize you and Amelia knew each other."

Sarah's eyes burned in the unwelcome warmth of Fran's face. She thought with dismay that she was probably the only person in the world who still blushed. Quelling the urge to explain, she said, "Hello, Fran. Rhea, how's the cardshark?"

"Do you know Mimi?" Rhea asked, her eyes glittering as she placed a hand on Mimi's arm.

Sarah shook Mimi's hand, wanting to break all the bones in it. The woman was a knockout, and she was apparently with Fran.

"Come play cards with me. Anytime." Rhea smiled a challenge.

"I will," Sarah said, wondering how many white lies she'd told under the guise of politeness.

As she and Amelia waited with Troy and Dale in the popcorn line, she threw furtive glances at the ticket counter. This was torment. Of course Fran would find someone else. But so soon? "I'll go get seats," she said, torn between wanting another glimpse of Fran and Mimi and the need to flee.

* * * * *

"What a small world it is," Mimi said. "I hope I don't see Bob — although he's probably home watching football."

Fran turned away. Her heart was thudding dangerously, seriously affecting her breathing. She'd seen the telltale red on Sarah's skin, a dead giveaway that Amelia was more than a friend. It made her want to change Realtors. No wonder Sarah had found somewhere else to live.

"I think I'm going to sit down on that bench over there," Fran's mother said, "while you two girls get the tickets." She rummaged in her purse, then gave up. "I'll pay you later, Franny."

"Don't worry about it, Mom." Instantly contrite, Fran was ashamed that she'd been only thinking about herself. "Go, sit."

"She gets tired quickly, doesn't she?" Mimi said.

"That's why we don't go many places. She'll probably fall asleep during the show."

A third of the way through the movie, her mother's head lolled forward. When her chin hit her chest, she straightened with a start, then slowly lapsed into sleep again.

Fran was sandwiched between her mother and Mimi, holding the box of popcorn so that they could share it. Two rows ahead sat Sarah with Amelia on her left and two men on the right. She noticed that Sarah spoke to the man next to her more than she did to Amelia. Unable to concentrate on the movie, she found herself unwillingly imagining Amelia and Sarah in compromising positions. The images made her squirm.

Mimi leaned toward her. "You okay?"

"I'm fine," she lied. It was easier not to see Sarah, not to know who she was spending her time with. It occurred to her that maybe the man next to Sarah was the one with whom she lived, the one she'd said she met up north. But where had she met Amelia, she wondered. She wanted the movie to be over, so she could get out of there.

When the lights came on, though, she saw that Sarah was apparently waiting for them by the doors to the small theater. She couldn't change direction because they were now closest to that aisle, so she waited while her mother slowly made her way into the flow of exiting people.

In the lobby, Sarah said, "These are my other friends, Troy and Dale."

They were strikingly good-looking men. Dale was thin-faced with dark hair and olive skin and nearly black eyes. He looked to be of Middle Eastern descent. Troy, on the other hand, could have posed for a Norman Rockwell cover with his black curly hair and soft brown eyes and open smile. This was the man Sarah was living with; she remembered his name.

"Troy wanted to meet you," Sarah explained.

Sarah had probably told him that Fran was her ex, and he was curious. Now she had two exes — Karl and Sarah. And no prospects in sight.

"Care to join us?" Troy asked. "We're going to the Dragon Gate for dinner."

Seeing the look Sarah shot at him, Fran knew it hadn't been her idea to invite them. "Thanks, but we're eating at Caesar's." She grabbed the name out of the air, panicked that he'd even suggest they have dinner together.

"We don't have a reservation," Mimi said.

"I think it'd be fun to eat together," her mother put in.

"There, you see," Troy said. "Two against one. Come with us."

Fran glanced despairingly at Mimi and her mother and then at Sarah, who seemed to be struck mute.

It was Dale who tried to save her. "Can't you see, Troy, that maybe they want to follow through with their plans?"

"We had no real plans," her mother said.

Fran could have popped her mother and strangled Mimi, who was smiling engagingly at the men. Couldn't she tell they were gay? Giving up, she said, "We'll meet you there."

The Dragon Gate was considered the best Chinese restaurant around. The parking lot was full, and the wind was sending gusts of rain across the blacktop.

"If it's too long a wait, we won't stay," Fran said.

"What's too long?" her mother asked as Fran helped her out of Mimi's Blazer.

Mimi held a puny umbrella over them as they hurried toward the door. "Half an hour," she said.

"Twenty minutes," the small, almond-eyed host promised.

When they ordered drinks from a table in the bar, Fran's mother requested a glass of red wine.

"You sure, Mom?"

"I'm positive, honey." She patted Fran on the arm. "I think it's time I started driving again too. We should go look at cars tomorrow."

This was serious. "We're moving closer to town, so you won't need a car, Mom."

"Then you don't have to pay for car insurance and license plates," Mimi said.

"We were at your open house last Sunday. Very nice," Troy remarked.

Surprised, Fran looked at Sarah for confirmation, but Sarah was staring fixedly at Troy.

When they were called to eat, Troy suggested ordering family style so that they could sample all the food.

"Where did you all meet?" Mimi asked brightly. Fran noticed that she'd shown particular interest in Dale, until he'd said he was a waiter by trade.

"I got to know Sarah and Troy on vacation this summer," Amelia said. "And you, do you and Fran work together?"

"We met through a mutual acquaintance," Mimi said, winking at Fran.

"Relationships are relationships," Fran's mother said, sipping her wine. "I used to think Sarah and Fran shouldn't live together."

"Troy and I lived together," Dale said. "We still do. Only now we're a threesome."

Fran realized from the expression on Mimi's face that she hadn't guessed. She felt wrung out, her armpits damp.

Sarah wrapped her fury at Troy around her and waited for an opportunity to express it. She and Amelia sat in the backseat as Troy's Explorer plowed through the heavy rain. Water sprayed out from under the wheels, and the wipers blatted back and forth trying to keep the windshield clear.

Amelia was saying, "Is Fran the one you left just before I met you?"

Sarah thought of what Fran's mother had said and turned her head toward the window to hide her smile. "Yes."

"Why didn't you say so?" Streetlights highlighted the planes of Amelia's face.

"I didn't want to talk about it. I still don't."

"You both looked so uncomfortable."

"I certainly was." Then she couldn't contain her anger any longer. "Why did you suggest we eat together, Troy?"

He said innocently, "Didn't you have a good time? I did. Fran's mother was delightful."

"I don't think Mimi knew any of us were gay. She was coming on to me," Dale said.

"You think everyone's coming on to you," Troy said with disgust.

"You think she's straight?" Sarah asked, wondering what Fran was doing dating a straight woman.

"She and Fran could just be friends," Amelia said.

Peering at the deserted streets, at the leaves falling under the onslaught of rain and wind, she wondered why that thought hadn't crossed her mind. It calmed her.

After they dropped Amelia at her condominium, Sarah leaned forward. "Don't do that to me again, Troy, or I won't go out with you."

"I'm sorry," he said, his teeth gleaming in the rearview mirror. "I thought it would give you a chance to see each other in a new light."

"I don't want to see her, period."

"The old lady looked like she was going to drop in her tracks by the end of the evening," Dale said. "That's the way I feel." He was leaning against the door.

"You shouldn't drink," Troy said, his grin gone. He stepped on the gas.

IX

Troy shook Sarah awake. "He's sick. Sweating like crazy, talking in his sleep, gurgling when he breathes."

She sat up and threw the covers off — then remembered she was in her bikinis and undershirt. Grabbing her sweats off the floor, she pulled them on. "Did you call a doctor?"

"He doesn't have a doctor. Besides, it's three o'clock in the morning."

"What do you want to do?"

"Go with me if I have to take him to ER."

She followed him down the hall. They passed Dale's doorway and turned into Troy's bedroom. "Why is he in your bed?" she asked, dumbfounded.

"He didn't want to sleep alone."

They stood whispering on the soft carpet next to the double bed.

Dale opened his eyes. "What are you doing staring at me?" He pulled the blankets up to his chin, then pushed them down. "God, I'm hot." He wore only boxer shorts.

She said, "Are you all right?"

"Would you be all right if you had HIV?"

Troy put a hand on Dale's forehead as he started to rise and pushed him down. "Go back to sleep. You're too feisty to be sick."

"Quit looking at me then."

Troy walked into the hallway with her. "Sorry. I panicked."

"Maybe he's got the flu, in which case he shouldn't be sleeping with you." She didn't get their relationship. "Maybe I shouldn't say this, but what you say doesn't match what you do, Troy."

"I know. I don't like sleeping alone."

"Here I thought you were such a tough guy."

"I am. Sorry I woke you." As she headed back to her room, he said, "I liked Fran. She loves you."

"Sure she does. That's why she's got a new girl-friend."

"I could tell by the way she looked at you."

She scoffed. "Like she wanted to run."

"Well, didn't you?"

"Yes," she admitted. "Now I'm going to bed. Don't wake me unless the house is burning down."

For a long time, she lay awake. Whenever a car

passed, its lights crossed the ceiling and walls of her room. The wind had died. She heard the rain rustling through the leaves, the sound of tires on wet pavement.

Her sleep was filled with unsettling dreams, starting with Fran's mother kissing her on the mouth and immediately turning into Amelia. Fran was furious. Then the scene changed and they were all in Dale's room, including Troy, watching Dale struggle to breathe. When Dale's face darkened, Troy asked if he should call an ambulance But she knew it was too late, that he would die before help could get there. Then her own mother appeared and advanced on the bed, saying she knew CPR. Troy said her mother shouldn't touch him. And she was indignant, telling him that she wouldn't hurt anyone, even though she realized her mother's touch would kill Dale.

The next morning Fran sat bathed in sunlight at the kitchen table, going through the real estate section of the classifieds. She planned to take her mother to open houses today. Mimi wanted to go with them. They would drive to Mimi's apartment and go in the Blazer.

She was circling an ad when her mother came into the room. "Coffee's on."

"It's a good day to look in the garage," her mother said.

Sunlight was unkind. It revealed the pink scalp under her mother's snow-white hair, diluted her blue eyes, and accentuated the wrinkles crisscrossing her cheeks. "The garage?"

"Yes, I want to go through my things."

"I thought we'd look at houses today."

"I'll have to have somewhere to put my car."

"Mom, your license isn't valid anymore. You don't want to spend money on a car. You might need it." The puppy was whining at the door, and she got up to let him outside.

"It's my money."

Fuck, she thought. Now what? "The car dealers aren't open on Sundays."

Her mother took the glass coffee pot off its heater, put it on the stove, and turned on the burner.

"Mom, what are you doing?"

"Heating up the coffee."

"It's already hot. The coffeemaker keeps it hot."

"We used to make it on the stove." Her mother sat down with a thud and began to cry.

Fran patted her on the back. "Don't, Mom." Tears were something she couldn't bear.

"I wasn't thinking. I'm sorry."

"It's okay. I'll fix breakfast." But the fear that her mother would burn the house down and herself with it filled Fran with apprehension.

"I'll make a note. It won't happen again." Getting the pad of paper next to the phone, her mother scribbled on it and stuck it to the coffeemaker. *Don't put coffee pot on stove.*

"Want to go fishing, cookie?" Troy suggested as they drank coffee and read the paper. "Your boat's getting flabby."

Sarah laughed. "What a good idea."

"I don't fish," Dale said, "but I can work on my tan."

Troy frowned. "Why don't you stay home and watch football?"

"If you don't want me along, just say so."

"Sure we want you to come. We'll make a picnic lunch." She gave Troy a warning look.

"Is Amelia coming?" Dale asked.

"She has two open houses," she said. It meant Sundays were her own, to spend as she pleased.

They put the boat in at one of the marinas. Sarah found herself perusing the people with a mixture of hopeful expectation and dread. Since she'd seen Fran at the theater, she expected to see her elsewhere. Dale held the boat at the dock while Troy loaded it with the tackle, bait, and the cooler. She parked the truck and walked to where they waited.

There was a slight wind, stirring the huge lake into movement. The sky was a perfect blue bowl, the sun warm, its rays bouncing off the glittering waves. Dale sat in the front, Troy behind her. She slowly drove the boat out of the channel, then pushed the lever to three-quarter throttle. This was the moment she loved — the rush of speed, the craft lifting itself out of the water, its bow rising, then leveling as it planed out.

Driving down the east side of the lake, she eased back the throttle north of Calumet County Park. It was then she noticed the wind was coming offshore. Surely more rain wasn't heading their way. At least they wouldn't be blown toward shore.

"I never fished this side of the lake," Troy said, dropping anchor when she turned off the motor.

Dale removed his shirt and stretched out across the bow. He watched them bait their hooks with worms and cast them into the water. "Why do you like to fish?"

Troy glanced at Sarah. "For me it's not knowing what I'm going to catch, the element of surprise and suspense."

"And being outside on the water while you're doing it," she added.

"I've done it in the water," Dale said with a grin.

Troy guffawed. "Betcha haven't done it in a boat."

"Bet I have."

Troy was obviously annoyed. "That's why you're in this fix; you've done it everywhere with everyone in every conceivable way."

"Come on, guys, not today, not in my boat," she said.

She lost track of time after a few hours. Although a thin haze of clouds covered the sky, the sun grew hot as the day wore on. They ate sandwiches when they were hungry and drank beer to quench their thirst. Dale fell asleep on the rocking prow as she and Troy caught one rock bass after another and threw them back in the lake. Troy was one fish ahead of her when she noticed the sun slipping toward the western shoreline and asked him the time.

"Can you believe it's after four already?"

"We better get off the lake before dark," she said.

The east banks were made up of parks, unlit by the cities and houses on the north and west and southern shores.

Dale awakened with a start when she turned the key.

Sandbars prevented them from hugging the shoreline. She had noticed the strengthening wind when they were anchored but hadn't felt its full power. Now out in the open, the waves washed over the bow as they plowed through the green-gray water. The boat rolled over a crest and dropped into a trough with a thud, only to rise and fall on the next wave.

They pulled on sweatshirts. No one had thought to bring a jacket. Troy, who had changed places with Dale, was soaked, and Sarah's face and hair were wet. There was no way she could go faster than half throttle, and she glanced at the rapidly vanishing sun with desperation.

She chided herself for forgetting how quickly bad weather changed the nature of this lake. The wind whipped its more than three hundred square miles of open water into a frenzy on short notice. Troy knew that too, yet they'd let the day get away from them.

Scared and cold, she turned the craft slightly northwest so that they would stop slipping over the waves. But with the wind behind them, the water began sloshing in over the stern. Dale hollered that they were going to sink.

"Flip the pump switch," she yelled.

"I'll do it." Troy crawled past her. "Keep going, cookie. We'll make it. But put this on anyway." He helped her into a life jacket, shrugged into one himself, and made Dale let go of the seat cushion long enough to don his. "Oh, to be a fish," he said, sitting on the floor between her and Dale, keeping watch over the pump.

The wind increased in volume, and she was forced to ride the crests and troughs of the waves again or they would take in too much water over the stern, lucky only that they were being pushed away from shore.

As the sun slipped out of sight, the lights of the marina showed her the way. They were close now, but her heart was in her throat for fear they would get caught on a sandbar or hit the rocks that formed a breakwater for the small harbor and channel. Only when they docked did she feel safe once more.

On the drive home, Troy put a hand on her knee. "Nice navigating, cookie. I never thought I'd appreciate dry land so much."

All she wanted to do was get home and call Fran. She'd wasted all this time, stupidly running away from what was good and right. Smiling at him, she glanced past him to Dale who looked wan under his tan.

"You want to go out with us next time, Dale?" she teased.

"Not on that lake," he said.

When they got home, she shut herself in the den, before Dale could stretch out on the couch and turn on the TV, and punched in Fran's number. "Come on, come on," she said as the phone rang three times.

"Hello, hello." She recognized Mimi's voice. "Anyone there?"

She quietly hung up the receiver. It would have been too humiliating to answer.

101

* * * * *

"Who was it?" Fran asked, her hands slimy with ground turkey.

"I don't know. Maybe it was Bob, spying on me," Mimi said.

"If you think that, you'd better get a restraining order."

"What's this note on the coffeemaker?"

"Mom put the coffee pot on the stove this morning to heat. The only good thing about it was that I think she realized that she shouldn't buy a car."

"I saw the notes on the bathroom mirror. They make interesting reading. Were they hers?"

"Yeah. She writes notes to remind herself to wash clothes, to fix dinner, to vacuum. I write notes to remind myself of appointments. Maybe it's not that much different."

Her mother had gone to lie down, taking Butch with her.

The phone rang again, and once more Mimi answered it. She covered the receiver and held it out to Fran. "It's a man asking for your mother."

"Probably my long-lost brother. Let me talk to him first." She wiped her hands on the dishrag and took the phone.

"Is Mom living with you, Fran?"

"She has been for weeks."

"I finally called the staff at Meadow Manor when she never answered her phone." His voice was accusatory. "Why didn't you tell me?"

"You didn't ask."

"She's not going back to Meadow Manor?"

"That's a dilemma. I have power of attorney, you know, and I've been paying her rent so that she won't lose the room there. Just in case she has to go back suddenly." She began to tell him some of the things that had happened. The notes, the afternoon her mother disappeared, the coffee pot on the stove, the imaginary animals that frequented her mother's room at night.

He was quiet, listening. But, in the end, he was no help. "You're closer to the situation. You'll have to decide when it's unsafe for her to live with you."

"Are you coming to visit her?"

"I want to pick her up the Saturday before Thanksgiving and bring her back the following Sunday, if that's all right."

Mimi went to tell Fran's mother to answer the phone, and Fran dug her fingers in the ground turkey again. Upon Mimi's return, she said, "Why do I get stuck with all the decisions and the work when she's his mother too?"

"Women are usually expected to be the caretakers. My sons are dropping by to see me and staying to dinner." Mimi sighed. "I think they miss the mothering."

"It's not that I don't want to care for my mother," she said. "I wouldn't want someone else to do it, but I'd like Matt to be more supportive and helpful. I wish he'd call her more and either visit or take her home for a few days every month. She thinks the sun rises and sets on him, and sometimes I get the feeling that I'm taken for granted."

"That's the reward for being boringly dependable."

"Do you think I'm boring?"

"I wouldn't spend so much time with you if I did. I do have some questions from last night, though," Mimi said. "Do you mind?"

Uh-oh, she thought. Here we go. "No."

"Sarah was your roommate?"

She put the Texas meatloaf into the oven. "Yes, for years."

"Are Troy and Dale gay?" Mimi took a pretzel out of a bowl and popped it in her mouth.

"I think so."

"And Amelia?"

"I don't know."

"Is Sarah?"

She turned toward Mimi, her face flushed with heat. "I am." Was it such a slur to admit that someone is gay that she hesitated to pin such a label on anyone?

"I didn't know." Mimi looked thoughtful. "Bob said you were."

"I can just hear him, telling you to stay away from that dyke."

Mimi laughed. "His words exactly."

"I don't bite, Mimi, nor am I interested in an intimate relationship with a straight woman."

"I know that. I feel so stupid."

She set the timer and leaned against the counter. "Why?"

"I don't know. I should have guessed." Mimi smiled crookedly. "Sorry about last night. Now I know why you didn't want to go out to eat with them. You still care about her, don't you?"

She ducked her head. "She left me, not vice versa."

"Maybe she was the one who called earlier. I shouldn't have answered the phone."

Fran snorted a laugh. "Fat chance."

Amelia called Sarah immediately after she hung up on Mimi.

"I'd love to come," Sarah said. Not true. She wanted to leave town, never risk seeing Fran and Mimi again.

She found Troy in the kitchen, getting leftovers out of the fridge.

"What do you say to a salad and warmed-up lasagna?" he asked.

"I'm not particularly hungry." The sound of the TV came from the den.

He put the food in the microwave. "Why the long face?"

"I'm going to Amelia's for dinner Friday night."

"Amelia's okay. You could do worse."

"I know."

He looked puzzled. "Is that who you called?"

"No. She's the one who called me. I phoned Fran."

"Did you talk to her?"

"I hung up when Mimi answered." She sat at the table and paged listlessly through the newspaper.

"Oh, and aren't we grown up. Why didn't you ask to talk to Fran?"

"She spends all her time with Mimi."

"And she no doubt thinks you do the same with Amelia," he said. "Cookie, you need a good fuck. You're too uptight."

"Oh, sure. That'll solve everything. And what about you?" It dawned on her then, and the effect was chilling. "You and Dale, you're not, are you? It's not safe."

"Sure it is."

"Then he doesn't have —"

"Who knows? He lies a lot. But I take precautions no matter what."

X

Amelia called Fran Monday evening. "The people who offered to buy your house accepted an offer on their house over the weekend."

Fran hadn't expected this. It would mean she'd have to find somewhere to live fast. Out of the three houses she'd looked at Sunday, there was one Cape Cod that she had liked. Not loved. The location was good, a nice neighborhood near the river and a park. Her mother had thought it was the house she'd lived in so many years, the one Fran had spent her childhood in. She told Amelia about it.

"I'll find out if there's an accepted offer on it. If not, you can make one. I'll call you first thing tomorrow evening."

When she hung up, Fran told her mother they would be moving soon.

"Where to, dear?"

"Remember that house we saw Sunday, the Cape Cod?"

"Our old house? Why did we leave it?" Her mother looked muddled.

She gave up. If her mother wanted to think it was their old house, what difference did it make. "I don't know, Mom." She'd call Amelia tomorrow and ask to see the house again.

Amelia was on the phone Friday night when Sarah arrived. "All right," she said into the receiver. "I'll try to set both closings for the morning of October 27." When she hung up, she smiled apologetically. "Sorry. That was Fran. She sold her house and bought another. I suppose you already know that."

Sarah didn't and wished the evening hadn't started this way. "No. I'm glad for her though."

"Well," Amelia said, rubbing her hands together, "let me have your jacket. I'll fix us a drink. What would you like? A mixed drink or wine?"

"Whatever you're having is fine."

"Wine then. Merlot okay?"

"Sure. Red wine's supposed to be good for you." She looked around as she followed Amelia's slender form to the kitchen. There were carpeted stairs going both down and up. On the main floor was the living room and kitchen. "Nice place. Interesting layout."

"Upstairs are the bedrooms and downstairs are a storage room and a large rec room. There are baths on all the floors. It suits me perfectly."

"You even have a fireplace in the living room."

"There's one downstairs too; they're both gas. No mowing grass or shoveling snow or hauling wood." She poured the wine. "Snacks are on the coffee table in the living room. Let's go sit and talk."

The living room contained an off-white davenport and easy chair, a glass-topped coffee table, and end tables with lamps. The carpet was light beige, the walls white. Brightly colored prints saved the room from starkness. She looked around for reading material and found none. Amelia was patting the sofa, so she sat next to her.

"I hear you barely made it to shore with your lives last Sunday."

"Yes. I thought we'd bought it." Putting a smoked herring on a cracker, she popped it in her mouth. "Mmm, good."

The light shed by the table lamps softened Amelia's features, making her dark skin glow. When she smiled, she looked provocative. "You know, it is so nice to be able to have a one-on-one conversation with you."

"I don't have a whole lot to say." She certainly couldn't share the debate she'd been having all week. Should she, shouldn't she, did she want to? Exasperated, Troy had said he'd never heard such agonizing over something that was supposed to be fun. He'd told her to go ahead and do it. If she didn't like it, she didn't have to do it again.

She expected to be able to wait until after dinner to make the final decision, but Amelia was edging toward her on the couch, encircling her with an arm when she leaned forward for a cheese and cracker.

"I'm always hungry afterward," Amelia said. "How about you?"

"What?"

Amelia laughed deep in her throat. "Come on, Sarah."

A surge of desire surprised Sarah, turning her legs and belly into warm mush. "Are we talking about sex before dinner or afterward?"

"I vote for now."

Climbing the stairs, Sarah experienced a moment of desperation, when she wanted to flee, and then it evaporated. Over a month had gone by since she'd last had sex and that had been with Amelia, unless she'd dreamt it.

"Why don't we just lie down together for a few minutes," Amelia suggested when they reached the bedroom.

"Sure." Looking around nervously, she was struck by how much the bedroom differed from the living room. Stacks of books and magazines cluttered the bedside table. They flowed onto the floor in an untidy heap. A forest green comforter covered the bed. The walls were decorated with framed photographs.

Amelia reached for her hand.

Sarah allowed herself to be drawn onto the bed. Now what? This was an old scene with a new twist. Facing Amelia, she thought how different Amelia appeared lying so close — more vulnerable, less manicured.

"I'm good at massages," Amelia said. "Turn over and I'll show you."

Obediently, Sarah rolled facedown.

"Let's take this off." Amelia tugged at Sarah's shirt, pulling it out of her slacks.

Unbuttoning the blouse, Sarah shrugged out of it, then placed her face on her crossed arms. Stiffening as Amelia undid her bra and straddled her hips, her muscles turned to jelly when strong fingers climbed her spine. Grunting under the manipulation, she wondered if this meant she'd have to massage Amelia in return.

"These too," Amelia said, snapping her waistband.

Raising herself, Sarah unzipped her pants and helped Amelia work them over her hips. Warmth flooded her.

"You have a nice body," Amelia said, gently kneading her behind, touching her intimately as if by accident.

She lifted herself to allow entrance. Excited, she moved against the long, slender fingers drawing pleasure from her.

After a few moments, though, she rolled on her back. She had always been the dominant sexual partner. "Lie down with me. Sex is something two people do together," she said.

Amelia shed her clothes without embarrassment. Her lean body was nicely molded. Even in the weak light her tan accentuated the white of her breasts and buttocks.

The lovemaking wasn't spectacular. They were too unsure of each other, too inhibited. Following the massage, nothing short of a knife to her throat could have kept Sarah from orgasm. She was surprised when Amelia came too and doubted it was the real thing.

"Now I want to see your reading material." Sarah leaned over the side of the bed and picked up a book.

Amelia said, "There's probably nothing you'd be interested in."

"Why not?"

"You're a librarian and a poet."

"Big deal. I read for entertainment."

"I'll go get dinner started." Amelia got up and put on a robe. "When you're ready, come on down.

It was her mother's fault that she was seldom able to be rude, she thought as she dressed after quickly reading through the titles. Instead of lying in bed enjoying a book as she wanted to, she was joining Amelia in the kitchen.

At dinner, Amelia's chenille bathrobe gaped whenever she leaned forward for a bite.

Sarah couldn't keep her eyes off the space between her breasts. Surprised by another flood of desire, she barely tasted the chicken divan.

"Can you stay the night?" Amelia asked.

"I didn't bring any clothes for work tomorrow." She'd thought she'd want to escape Amelia, not sleep with her.

"Tomorrow's Saturday."

"I had last weekend off."

Fran had a month to box, but she started going through her dresser drawers Friday night. Surrounded by mementos of her children's early years, she sat on the bed and looked through their old report cards, smiled at their drawings and the stories they'd created for classes. She paged through photo albums that recorded their growing years. It made her long to see them.

Thinking perhaps they'd come for one of the holidays, she called them in order of their births — Jay first. He was working the days after Thanksgiving and Christmas.

"Visit me anyway, Mom. I'll show you a good time."

Why not, she thought. She had the money, she had vacation time, and otherwise she'd be alone over Thanksgiving.

With misgivings, she pushed in Chelsey's number. Although she called both of her kids regularly, she never knew what kind of reception she'd get from her daughter.

"Hi, Mom. What's up?"

She told Chelsey about the upcoming move, how her grandmother thought they were moving back home.

"Grandma's not doing so well, is she?"

"She's slipping. She'd love to see you; so would I."

"I can't afford to fly home, Mom."

"If I sent you the plane fare, would you come for Christmas?" What else did she have to do with her money anyway?

"That'd be a neat present. I have to talk to Jamie Lynn first, though."

"Maybe she'd like to come with you."

"Thanks, Mom. I'll ask her and get back with you."

She put the keepsakes in a box, annoyed that Chelsey couldn't make a decision on her own.

Troy looked up from the book he was reading in the living room when Sarah returned home late Friday night. "How was it?"

"What are you anyway, my mother?" she asked, remembering how her mother had waited for her to return home nights during her teen years. It had been like running the gauntlet. Too often she'd been drinking or necking and was unable to pass muster. Tonight she would have welcomed even her mother's sharp eye and discerning nose just to have her around again.

"Come on, don't keep me in suspense." He wore a chenille bathrobe like Amelia's, only dark brown. His chest hairs sprouted out of its opening.

"You were right; I needed a fuck." In fact, she felt relaxed and grateful toward Amelia.

"Was it good?" he asked, a wide smile dimpling his cheeks.

Shrugging, she sat on the chintz couch next to him. "It was okay. I don't know about you, but it takes time for me to get used to someone."

He frowned in thought. "Maybe it's different."

"Anyway, what's it to you?"

He patted her on the leg. "I've been worried about you, girlfriend."

She laughed. "I'm going to bed. I have to work tomorrow."

XI

Fran had set the moving day for October 28. It hadn't given her time to paint or to clean the carpets in the new house, but she had to vacate the log house after closing, and she couldn't get into the Cape Cod until it was officially hers.

Mimi was helping with the move, so was Nina and her partner, Jaclyn. She needed muscle, but she couldn't ask Bob. Mimi volunteered her sons yet Fran hesitated to accept, sure that Bob would get wind of the move.

She wouldn't call on old friends whom she'd

virtually ignored since her breakup with Sarah. She lived too far out to maintain some of those friendships, and seeing them reminded her of Sarah. There was only so much time to see people, and a lot of hers was taken up by her work, by her mother, by Mimi.

When the phone rang the night before the move, she was sitting in the TV room with her mother wondering how they were going to pick up the furniture, especially the antiques. The rented moving truck was parked outside the garage.

"Hi. Remember me? Troy Buchanan? I heard you were moving tomorrow. I called to offer my services and Dale's."

For a moment she scanned her memory and up he popped. Sarah's friend. She couldn't believe her luck and said warily, "Here I was wondering how we were going to lift some of these things, and out of the blue you call."

"Telepathy," he said with a laugh. "Then you do need a man. We are good for something."

"Oh, yes," she said. "Who told you?"

"Amelia."

Did Sarah know? She hadn't offered to help. Maybe she would show up. "That was nice of her," she said.

The next morning Fran was up at six, rousing her mother so that she would have time to shower and dress.

"Where are we going?" her mother asked.

"We're moving today, Mom. Everybody will be

here at seven." Over the weeks she had readied herself for this day and, now that it was here, she wondered why she didn't feel more emotion.

Bounding down the stairs with Butch yapping at her heels, she opened the door to cool sunlight. Blue jays screeched in the pines, and she knew that whenever she heard their calls she would think of the log house. It was the scenario that had caused her to fall in love with this location. Steeling herself, she recalled the cold, snowy nights when the roads were barely negotiable, remembered the isolation and loneliness after Sarah's leave-taking.

Turning the truck around, she started loading boxes from the garage. Some of her mother's things were here. Maybe there'd be room in this new house for at least a few of them. She should ask whether she would have to pay the nonrefundable entry fee again if she let the room go at Meadow Manor and put her mother on a waiting list. It wouldn't hurt to inquire. Having made the decision to get more information, she felt as if a weight had lifted off her.

"Why don't you bark when you're supposed to?" she asked Butch when a horn startled her. Instead, he barked when somebody ran or when they refused to move and he wanted them to.

Mimi jumped out of her Blazer. "Sorry. My elbow hit the horn." Standing in the open garage doorway, she looked around. "There are other people helping, aren't there?"

"Yep. See." Fran pointed as Nina parked her Dodge van behind Mimi's Chevy, followed by Troy in his Explorer.

Troy had come alone, explaining that Dale didn't feel well. He galloped up the stairs, took one end of the heaviest furniture while Nina, matching muscles, picked up the other. Together they staggered down the steps to the truck. Then they went back for another piece, teasing and challenging each other.

"You're going to get a matched set of hernias," Fran said after a while, hoping they wouldn't wear out before everything was set up in the new house. "Why don't you stop for a minute for coffee and doughnuts?"

"I'll be fine," Troy crowed. "I've got my belt on." He showed them a wide band strapped around his middle.

"I've got mine on too," Nina said, snapping her bra and laughing.

When the truck was loaded, Fran walked through the empty rooms. She heard echoes of her children, her ex-husband, of Sarah. She made a last phone call to the cleaning service she had hired so that she wouldn't have to return to do that herself. Then she closed and locked the door behind her, leaving a key under the mat.

They caravaned to the new house, and she sent Mimi to get pizza for lunch. Everyone fell on the food as if they were starved — including her mother, who saved the crusts for Butch. The dog was in the fenced-in backyard, his barks occasionally rising to yowls. No doubt he thought he was abandoned.

By late afternoon the truck and other vehicles were unloaded, and the rooms were littered with boxes that needed emptying. The beds were set up, the fridge loaded with food, the furniture in place.

Fran's mother wandered through the new house.

In the kitchen she said to Troy, "Matt, help me look for your dad."

Fran looked up from the box she was unpacking, her insides chilling. "This is Troy, Mom, not Matt."

"Troy? Are you Matt's friend?"

He smiled kindly. "Matt isn't here, Rhea, nor is his dad. There's just us, and we'll have to make do without them."

Mimi glanced at Fran and then at her mother. "You must be tired, Rhea. Why don't you help me make the beds?"

When Mimi had gone off with her mother, Fran sighed. Maybe buying this house had been a mistake. Her mother might spend her days searching for her father and Matt.

After work Saturday, Sarah found Dale in the den watching a football game. "You sure are a big sports fan."

"Wouldn't you be if those were girls galloping up and down the field? Look at that quarterback's cute little ass."

"Look at those fat defensive tackles. Where's Troy?"

"He tried to rope me into helping your old girl-friend move."

"What?" She felt betrayed. Why hadn't he told her?

Dale shouted encouragement to a running back who had just caught the ball. Then said, "Yep. He called her and offered our help without even consulting me. Ballsy, huh?"

"But you didn't go."

"Nope. I told him I didn't feel good. I have to work later anyway."

"I'll be gone overnight. Tell him if you see him, will you?" She started toward her room.

"Say hello to Amelia," he called after her.

Climbing the stairs, she wondered if she would have felt compelled to help had she known Fran was moving. Seeing Mimi would start up those dark feelings again. And what right did she have to be jealous, she was fucking Amelia.

She let herself into the condo with the key Amelia had given her. A fire was burning on the gas grate in the living room. She walked the hall to the kitchen, thinking that she'd begun last night as a guest and was now someone who belonged.

"Did you tell Troy that Fran was moving today?"

Amelia turned from the stove to look at her. "Yes. I figured she might need help."

"You didn't tell me."

"Why would I? Want to make a salad?"

She went to the fridge for the makings and carried them to the cutting board. "I would have helped too."

"That's why I didn't tell you. I'm not that much of a fool. Although if you want to go back to Fran, I won't try to stop you."

As Sarah tossed her jacket on a chair, the doorbell rang.

"That'll be Candy and Georgie. I invited them to dinner. Hope you don't mind. Can you get the door?"

She felt weird, letting them in, taking their coats, getting them a couple of cold beers as if she lived here. Leaning on the counter while she and Amelia fixed dinner, they ate chips and salsa and drank.

"Have you been writing?" Candy asked her.

"I set up my computer when I moved in with Troy," she said wryly, thinking she hadn't written a letter on it, much less anything creative.

"There's a writers' group forming. They're all lesbians or gay men. Georgie's joining it." Candy shot a smile at her lover.

"I didn't know you wrote, Georgie." But then she'd never asked.

Georgie blushed. "I haven't published anything."

Candy nudged her. "Don't be so modest. She writes short stories and essays."

"Would you like to go with me?" Georgie asked.

Maybe it would force her to write again. "Sure."

In bed that night, unable to sleep, she stared at the ceiling. All of a sudden she couldn't wait to get to her computer, and she lay listening to Amelia's steady breathing for what seemed hours.

In her room the next day, Sarah faced her monitor and poured her thoughts out to its screen. *Letters to Loved Ones,* she titled the script.

> *You were my first love, Mom, the recipient of my first smile, my first words. I vied with my sisters for your attention. Standing on my hands in the water, performing somersaults*

across the lawn, drawing pictures, I called, "Look, Mom, look."

When I was eight, Mom, I wanted to be a cowboy. I rode my horse alongside the car wherever we went, galloping through ditches, jumping fences, unafraid of speed or falling. At home I rode through the neighorhood, my bike a steed. Striding through the house, I dressed in imaginary chaps and boots and cowboy hat. It was a black-and-white world. I worshiped you.

At thirteen, Mom, I bought you an electric frying pan for Christmas. I walked downtown alone one cold Friday night and made my purchase, spending what for me was a lot of money. My heart was in that gift. Why I thought you'd be so happy to receive a frying pan I don't know. What I recall is the snowy night and the heady pleasure of buying you something so pricey.

On my eighteenth birthday, Mom, I told you about my girlfriend. I saw the different shades of your skin. You paled, then flushed, otherwise registering no surprise. "I think I knew," you said, but didn't explain how. I was left feeling oddly deflated. Were you disappointed? Did my sisters gain stature in contrast?

Struggling for independence from loving you too much, I drew battle lines and then surrendered. Our discussions were sometimes heated, Mom, so sure in my arrogant youth that I was right. We laughed more as we grew older, sometimes clutching for control.

Did you know I was there when you died, Mom? Your eyes were closed. I heard your uneven breathing, saw your hands move in distress. The doctor told me to call you back. I did, feebly, not at all convinced that it would work or that you wanted to live. Now I call when I'm alone. I shout, "Mom, are you there? Do you hear?"

I miss you.

She grabbed a tissue, wiping her eyes and blowing her nose. Knowing she couldn't read this to a group, she began again — this time fictionalizing a dilemma and a character.

Troy's knock startled her out of the world she'd created. Refocusing slowly, she noticed the room growing dark around her. Saving what she'd written, she invited him in.

"I hear I'm up shit creek," he said.

She hadn't seen him since Thursday night. Caught between the real world and the world of her imagination, the real world seemed irrelevant. She gazed at his rosy face. "How did the move go?"

"You'd already left for Amelia's when I asked Fran if she needed help," he said.

"You don't have to answer to me."

Sitting on the bed, he bounced a little. "She needed a man. Nina and Jaclyn weren't enough."

"And Mimi?"

"She's stronger than I thought," he said. "What have you been doing in here all afternoon?"

"Writing." She'd rediscovered an escape mechanism. "Where'd she move?" Was she living with Mimi now? She couldn't ask.

He told her. "Come on, girlfriend. Supper's ready.
I want to hear about your weekend."

The weekend had proved more confusing for
Fran's mother. Late in the afternoon Sunday, she
gave out treats for Halloween. Fran hovered behind
her, holding the candy dish and listening.

"Do you know Franny and Matt? They go to
Nicolet," her mother asked the first group of kids.

When they left, she said, "Mom, Nicolet's not a
neighborhood school, and I'm Fran."

"Your name's Fran, too?"

Butch had tried to shove his way outside, leaping
for the candy, attempting to lick the trick-or-treaters.
It was cold, and wind swept through the open door.
She took him by his collar and shut him in the
kitchen, where he yowled and scratched at the door.

She was tired, having spent the day unpacking
boxes. Her mother had left a burner on, making her
realize that she would have to return home over the
noon hour, but she was close enough to do that now.
And on top of it all, apparently her mother thought
she was still a kid.

"Fran, where's the candy?"

Ridiculously grateful to be recognized, she laughed
at herself.

XII

Fran's brother, Matt, arrived late morning the Saturday before Thanksgiving. He and his wife admired the new house, drank a cup of coffee, bundled Fran's mother into their Buick Riviera, and left. With Butch whining anxiously beside her, Fran stood at the door watching the car back out of the driveway. Her mother, who looked tiny sitting in the backseat, had sung Matt's praises earlier. She was so excited about going to his house that Fran was unpleasantly surprised by old jealousy. She'd wanted to say, *Wait a minute, Mom, what about me? I care for you every day. Matt comes and gets you a couple times a year and you think he can do no wrong?*

It wasn't fair, of course. It seemed to her that the child, usually a daughter, who assumed the caretaker role was unappreciated. It was the more distant offspring who was praised for whatever slim efforts he or she made.

She called Mimi and asked her over for dinner, saying, "I'm a little blue."

"So am I, Fran. My kids are here, watching football. I think I'll throw them out and come over now, if you don't mind."

When Mimi arrived, they walked Butch to the park by the river. Chunks of ice raced by on the current. Ducks and geese bobbed in the open water. A cutting wind lifted their hair and reddened their cheeks. Butch shivered at the end of the leash, his tail tucked between his legs. After a few minutes, they hurried home.

They hauled in wood and built a fire. Fran put on some CDs while Mimi made hot chocolate. Sitting on the couch, hands warming around their cups, they watched the fire take hold. The yellow flames licked at the kindling, then turned red and blue as they began gobbling the split oak.

"I'll miss you over Thanksgiving weekend," Mimi said.

Fran, who was rediscovering contentment, murmured, "You'll be busy with your family."

Mimi grimaced. "Lucky me. My sons and their girlfriends, my parents and Bob. Why am I expected to spend my holidays acting as if I never left Bob?"

"What would you like to do?"

"Go somewhere warm and exotic, and if I can't do that, take in a movie."

"You could go see something, you know, while the others watch football. Would you like to fly to Mexico with me next year and forget about Christmas?"

"Would I ever."

Butch leaped to his feet and the doorbell rang, in that order.

Fran wasn't expecting anyone and said with mild surprise, "I wonder who it is?"

Mimi, however, looked alarmed. "If it's Bob, don't let him in."

"It's not Bob," she said. But it was. She could see him through the thick glass pane in the door.

"Don't open it," Mimi warned.

"I won't let him in," Fran promised, unlocking the deadbolt and cracking the door a few inches. "What do you want?"

The flat of his hand slammed against the steel panel, nearly knocking her off her feet. Stunned, she watched him cross the living room toward Mimi in a few strides. Barking and snarling, Butch snapped at his pantlegs. The pup yipped in surprise when he was sent flying by the heel of a Wellington boot.

"She's seduced you, hasn't she? That's what they do, you know, try to corrupt normal people." He grabbed Mimi's arms and shook her. "Wake up, you stupid woman. She's a dyke, she wants you. I love you."

Mimi tried to wrench herself free. "This is what you call love. You break into someone's house and attack them."

"You're coming with me." He started dragging her toward the door.

"Call the police," Mimi yelped.

In a daze, Fran picked up the phone and punched in 911. But before she could speak, Bob knocked the receiver out of her hand. At the same time, he threw Mimi down with disgust.

"All right. I'm going. But I won't put up with this." He clumped outside.

Quickly closing the door, Fran locked it. Her hands shook. "I'm calling the police anyway."

"He's gone," Mimi said.

"I don't care." Belatedly furious at the intrusion, the real and implied violence, she picked the phone off the floor. Looking around for Butch, she asked, "Where's the dog?"

Mimi found him in the downstairs bedroom under Fran's mother's bed, and coaxed him out. "I'd hide too. What a brute. I'm sorry, Fran."

Scooping the puppy into her arms, Fran said, "The police are coming over. We'll have to make a statement. Think about getting a restraining order, Mimi. I worry about you." She worried about her own self too.

"He always tried to keep me away from other people," Mimi said. "Fuck him. I'm not going to do what he wants anymore."

After the police left, they ate and watched a video. Fran asked Mimi if she wanted to spend the night, but Mimi said no.

"Call me," she said when Mimi left. She double-checked the locks on all the doors and windows before climbing the stairs with the pup on her heels.

* * * * *

Wednesday after work Mimi took Fran to the airport. She was flying via O'Hare to Orlando, where Jay, whom she hadn't seen since last January, would be waiting. Fran never realized how much she missed her kids until she was going to see one of them again. Then she allowed herself the luxury of anticipation, of excitement.

Her visits with her children were never as she expected them to be. Chelsey usually kept Fran at arm's length, showing mild skepticism over her opinions. Although affable, Jay seldom let her into his life. More often than not, he seemed preoccupied, making her feel like a distraction. Afterward, she often felt empty and frustrated. She longed to have a real conversation with them, to exchange thoughts and feelings. Instead, they acted as if her ideas were criticisms. If she threw something controversial at them, they became defensive.

When she spied Jay in the waiting crowd, a ball cap perched on his dark hair, she felt suddenly shy. He smiled and waved, and her heart thumped harder. She remembered him as a small boy, grinning and waving wildly when he spied her in the Little League stands.

"Hey, Mom. How are ya?"

She'd forgotten how big he was, over six feet, with broad shoulders and narrow hips. Engulfed in his hug, she felt small. Backing off, she said, "Let me look at you," and noted that he was heavier, no longer boylike.

He looked down at her, a silly grin on his face. "You're so tiny. How's Grandma? How was the flight?"

She smiled teasingly. "Whoa. One question at a time. First let's go get my bag." Her carry-on was a backpack, which he took off her shoulder.

Keeping an arm around her, he walked her to the baggage carousel. "We're going straight to the store," he said. "I want an old-fashioned Thanksgiving dinner."

"We can do that, if you promise to help." He, not Chelsey, had always been her assistant in the kitchen. His sister scorned cooking, while he enjoyed it.

"I'll do the pies, the potatoes, the veggies, and fruit salad if you'll do the dressing and turkey and rolls."

"Fair enough." Maybe they would talk. "Is anyone else coming for dinner?"

"You always were psychic." Long hair curled from under the back of his cap. His blue eyes were a reflection of her own. "Her name is Katie. I'm in love, Mom."

She smiled to hide her disappointment. She had hoped not to share him these few days.

"She lives with me. I didn't want to tell you. I was afraid you wouldn't come. She's going to her parents' Friday for the weekend. She wanted to meet you first."

Already she liked the girl better for giving her time alone with him. She pointed at the belt. "That's my bag."

He snatched the suitcase and set it down. "What have you got in here? Sand?" His grin was contagious.

She shrugged sheepishly. "Sorry." She never knew what to pack, so she took as much variety as the suitcase would hold, even though she never wore most of it.

Hot sunshine poured in on a warm breeze through the windows of Jay's beat-up Chevy 1500 truck. "How's the job?"

After struggling through two years of college, he had sailed through two years at the Tech. He worked in a store that sold small engines and equipment. "I'm saving my money. I want to buy the place someday."

Patting him on the leg, she said, "Good. That's the way to get ahead."

"How's Sarah?" he asked.

To her the question came out of the blue, and this time she was surprised by the lack of pain. "She moved out."

"Did someone else move in?" He was staring out the windshield, dodging in and out of lanes as if in a terrible hurry.

"Your grandma and Butch." She winced at the memory of leaving Butch at the kennel, his forlorn gaze following her out the door. How could he know she was coming back?

"Butch is the dog?" When she nodded, he said, "You didn't say how Grandma was."

"She's getting a little short in the memory department."

"Tell her to hang in there. I want her to come to my wedding."

She smelled the saltwater when they neared the small white stucco house about two miles from the Gulf. Jay parked in the driveway, grabbed her suitcase out of the covered truck bed, and followed her to the front door.

The girl who opened the door was like no one she expected to see. Jay had always pined after short pretty girls. Katie wore glasses and was tall and thin and plain. Later Fran understood the appeal when she discovered the young woman was witty and smart and kind. She was proud of her son for looking at more than appearance.

"How did you meet?" she asked when they sat down to the pizza they'd ordered.

Their mouths full, the two young people looked at each other and smiled. Katie swallowed and spoke first.

"I was going to the university and working part-time doing the books where Jay works. He'd come in every morning hungover and tease me about my lack of a life." Katie scowled at him. "As if that was a life, chasing girls and drinking."

"She always had her nose in a book, like you, Mom," Jay cut in. "I decided to give her a thrill and asked her out. She turned me down."

"Then I was a challenge, I guess. He doesn't like being spurned."

"We started a conversation. It hasn't ended," he said. "Mom, she knows that you and Sarah are together."

Fran blushed. She wasn't ready for confidences with this young woman she'd just met. And she'd never disclosed herself to her son. "Oh, well. We aren't anymore."

Amelia left for her parents' home Wednesday

afternoon. Dale drove to Milwaukee to spend the weekend with his parents. Sarah was going nowhere, although both her sisters had invited her to their houses.

"Don't leave," Troy begged her. "My dad will be thrilled. He'll think I've gone straight."

She was baking when he left to meet his parents' incoming flight Wednesday evening. The pies were cooling on the counter, and she was reading in the den when he returned with his folks.

Troy introduced her as his roommate.

"Hello, dear. You're a nice surprise," his mother said. "Call me Eleanor." She was a petite, feminine version of Troy, her eyes pools of chocolate in a creased, tanned face.

His father, Nathan, shook her hand and growled, "Smells good in here." He loomed over his wife, both of them spare and fit looking. Golfers or walkers, she assumed. If his mother had given Troy his looks, his father had passed on his build.

"Can we eat one of the pies?" Troy asked.

"Why not?" she said.

Thursday morning his mother confided to her over a cup of coffee. "I know you and Troy are just friends, Sarah. You don't have to put on an act for me. Where is Dale anyway?"

"Home with his family."

"Isn't it sad that they can't go together?"

She didn't think Troy wanted to go home with Dale, but she only listened.

"We joined P-FLAG when we found out about Troy. Nathan didn't do well with it. He said he was afraid that if he was understanding, Troy would put on dresses. I think I always knew. Troy was such a gentle, kind little boy. His brothers were brutes in comparison."

Looking up, Eleanor greeted Troy and her husband. "Hello, dears. Sleep well? Sarah and I were having a heart-to-heart."

"About us, I suppose," Troy said, grinning suddenly.

His mother winked at Sarah. "Don't be so conceited."

Over the next few days, she got to know his parents well enough to relax around them. His father was austere with a dry sense of humor, but his mother made her collapse with laughter. She drove to the airport with them when they left Sunday afternoon. And on the way home, she said, "I'd marry you, Troy, for your mother."

He turned to grin at her. "Want to go home with me for Christmas? You're invited."

"Will your brothers be there?"

"Does it matter? We'll blow them away."

"I don't want to be part of a farce."

A cold sun lit his face. "What's wrong with taking a friend home for the holidays? People do it all the time."

XIII

Snow started falling Sunday after midnight and continued into Monday. Fran drove through a thickening veil of white with tires whirring. She measured the growing depth on her boots at each stop. A cutting wind picked up in the afternoon, flinging the snow sharply against the windshield, little knives slicing her face whenever she stepped outside to deliver.

Her mother was at Meadow Manor, where her brother had left her on Sunday. Mimi had met her at the airport at eight that evening, but she'd been so tired she had gone home and straight to bed. The dog was still at the kennel. She wondered whether her mother or the dog knew that she was coming for them after work.

She grocery shopped over her noon hour, racing through the aisles at Woodman's. If she hadn't had a list, she would have bought whatever looked good because she was hungry. Putting the bags of food in the step-van, she continued her deliveries while eating a bagel and a banana. The roads were slippery, and even the smallest skid sent her heart marching into overtime. She could get fired for an accident. Then what would she do?

Considering the question, she wondered if it was too late to go back to a sit-down job. She'd majored in business, had worked in a credit union first as a teller, then as a loan officer. The pay was piss poor, and she'd hated being cooped up. And when Karl left her, she'd needed more income. Chelsey had asked why she didn't have a job like other mothers, why she had to drive a truck like a man.

Ten years from now, though, she might not want to be out in the cold all winter. The snow was coming down thick, and she shivered whenever she stepped outside. Her clothes steamed inside the van. Glancing at herself in the mirror, she saw her plastered hair framing a reddened face. Already Florida was a dream and Jay a memory.

When the day ended and she jumped into her truck to fetch the dog before the kennel closed, she was exhausted. She asked for Butch and heard his joyous, answering barks from the maze of cages within. Like a small sled dog, he dragged the girl at the end of his leash through the waiting-room door.

Fran laughed as he jumped on her in jubilant welcome.

"We have dog obedience classes here," the girl said.

"When he's old enough," Fran replied.

From the kennel she drove to Meadow Manor, where she took Butch to her mother's room. He shied away from the papery hands that reached for him on the way, from the wavery voices that cooed, "Isn't he adorable?"

He was cute, she realized, stopping and stroking him so that others could do the same. When he was lying in a ball, it was hard to tell which end was the front. But standing, his tail curled over his back and his small pink tongue pointed out his mouth. Sheltered by long brows, his large brown eyes peered out from a black, curly coat.

She found her mother asleep on her bed, her suitcases unpacked in a corner. Before she could waken her, Butch jumped at the bed with a whine and a bark. Her mother's eyes flew open wide, for a moment vacant and startled.

"Hi, Mom. It's just me and Butch. Sorry. Didn't mean to surprise you."

Swinging her legs over the side of the bed, her mother sat up and tried to pet the dog, not an easy feat since he was behaving like a yo-yo. "What a nice dog? What's his name?"

"You named him Butch, Mom. Remember?"

"Butch. Yes."

Fran talked to the staff and gathered her mother's suitcases. "Let's go home, Mom."

* * * * *

Sarah worked Monday night. She was at the reference desk in the middle of the library's main floor when Amelia showed up, snow dusting her shoulders and hair.

"Hi," she said, looking up with surprise.

"I've decided to get my books from the library. What do you think?"

"Saves money."

Amelia's voice dropped. "Can you come over tonight? I missed you over the weekend."

Sarah had writing she wanted to work on for tomorrow night when the writer's group met at Georgie's house. "Wednesday," she promised and added, "I missed you too," slightly stunned to realize that she had.

Candy and Georgie lived in a two-bedroom flat in a large old house across from a park. Sarah rang the doorbell, then bounded up the steps. Georgie took her coat and introduced her to the other six people — three men and three women. Candy was nowhere in sight.

Sarah was nervous and clutched her story to her chest as if afraid someone might snatch it away. Actually, she was too distracted to know what she was doing.

Troy had teased her at supper. "What's the matter, cookie? You act like you got a hot date, not a meeting with a bunch of aspiring writers."

"I'll have to read what I've written." Except when she'd had to read aloud in class, she'd never read her writing to anyone.

"Why did you write it if you don't want it read?"

"I do want it read. I just don't want to be around when somebody reads it."

"You are so silly."

"Is Dale at work?" she asked.

"Yep. Miss him?" He buttered a roll and took a bite.

"I know he's gone." Mostly because the TV was off. She spooned cream of broccoli soup into her mouth.

He cocked an eyebrow and pointed the roll at her. "Not the same thing. What's your story about?"

"Your mother."

He perked up. "Can I read it?"

"Later," she'd promised.

Lloyd, a heavy man who was scrunched at one end of the couch next to two skinny guys, was talking — telling them that he thought this group should offer constructive criticism on members' writings read at meetings: a chapter, a short story, a poem. "Looks like you brought something," he said to Sarah.

She jumped. "Yes."

"Why don't you read it to us? Don't be shy."

"Well." She cleared her throat, her pulse thrumming in her ears.

A murmur of encouragement rose from the group encircling Georgie's living room.

As she read, the flush suffusing her face subsided bit by bit until she thought it was gone. But when the group began making suggestions, the blood flowed back until her eyes burned in its heat.

"I think it's a good start," Lloyd said. "You've given us a picture of this woman, you just need to flesh her out. If you made copies, we could follow when you read."

Her hands and pits were sweaty, and she felt drained as if she'd done something strenuous.

A woman named Joy told her not to worry about what anyone thought — her relatives, her friends — or she'd never write anything worthwhile. Then, with only a slight, telltale blush, Joy read a sensual poem about a woman and her lover in bed together.

Georgie went next with a thinly disguised story about her life with Candy. The writing was so rhythmic that Sarah felt rocked by it. It was beautiful but threatened to put her to sleep. She remembered an English instructor telling the class to use action verbs and vary the structure and length of sentences. Tactfully, she passed on this information.

The next woman read an essay, as did each of the two skinny men. One of the essays was very funny. Then Lloyd, who wanted to go last, gave them a sex scene. She was appalled by the detail.

Lloyd laughed into the stunned silence that followed. "Look, I know it's porn. That's what I write. Like Joy said, you can't worry about what people think. I need you to tell me: A, Does it hold your interest? And B, Can you picture what I've written?"

"I can," Joy admitted. "But sex is more exciting if you leave something to the imagination. Are you writing a manual or are you writing fiction? You can't do both at once."

"It sells," Lloyd said. "Anyone else?"

It was an unfitting end to the evening, Sarah thought, afraid to confess that what he'd written offended her.

At home, Troy pressed her to show him the story

about his mother. "When it's revised," she said. "One guy read a piece of pornography."

"Tell me about it." He was lying on the couch in his robe, an open book in his lap.

She sat next to his feet, one leg on the cushion, and thought about dripping penises inserted into hairy anuses. "It curled my lip."

He grinned and scratched his head. "Not mine, I bet."

"I'm going to bed and dream about oral sex."

He looked up at her as she stood and stretched. "Was any of it kinky?"

"Fisting, cock rings. I'd have to say yes."

"Some do, most don't, but we like to read about it occasionally. I've heard of Lloyd. He does sell that stuff. Girls do some of those things too, you know."

"I know. It caught me by surprise. He's sort of the mouthpiece for the group. I expected to hear something literary."

After work on Wednesday Sarah drove to Amelia's, where she told her about the writers' session over dinner. They were finishing the wine in their glasses. Candlelight flickered over their faces.

Amelia asked, "Would you like to try some toys?"

Curious, she said, "Do you have any?"

"One or two. I'll show them to you later." Amelia grinned and winked.

A familiar heat flooded her. She realized that her feelings for Amelia had more to do with sex than love.

When they climbed into bed, Amelia opened a bedside drawer and took out a plastic bag.

"Are the toys in there?" Huddling under the covers, Sarah wished she hadn't asked about them. She took the bag and peered inside, seeing a vibrator and a dildo with an attached thumb. "I don't think so," she said.

Amelia shrugged and put them back. "We don't need them. Sometimes it's fun to experiment." She smiled and reached for Sarah. "Let me show you how much I missed you."

It was easy to succumb to Amelia's passion. To be desired was a form of seduction. And Amelia made it very clear that she wanted her.

"I get wet just looking at you," Amelia said. "Do you know that?"

Wrapping her legs around Amelia's spare frame, Sarah rocked with her.

Amelia pushed her hair back and brushed her face with kisses. "I'm crazy about you, Sarah."

Unable to parrot Amelia's affections, she responded instead with action. Before she could roll Amelia over, though, she felt a cool thickness between her legs. Stiffening, she paused long enough for penetration. It reminded her of her youth, when she'd used zucchinis and cucumbers and roll-on deodorant containers to get the same effect.

"I thought we weren't going to do this," she said.

Amelia smiled down at her and flipped the switch.

The effect was instantaneous satisfaction, which was over just as quickly. She was left lying weakly in a pool of desire.

"Well, did you like it?" Amelia asked.

"What's to like? I never came so fast in my life."

A sense of fair play forced her to struggle up off her back. "Give me that," she said, grabbing the dildo. Almost angrily she thrust it into Amelia and watched the results with amazement.

Afterward, she felt cheated.

XIV

She was a daughter, a friend, a mother in that order, Fran thought. Partner, lover, other half, significant other didn't apply to her anymore. "Aren't you lonely?" she asked Mimi one Saturday in mid-December when they were Christmas shopping in the mall.

"Yeah," Mimi replied. "I've even considered going back to Bob."

"What?" Fran stopped in her tracks, while the flow of people parted around them.

"Don't worry. It was just a momentary weakness."

"You'd never get away if you went back."

"I know. Credit me with a few smarts." Mimi took Fran's arm and forced her to continue walking. "I'm horny, is all. You take sex for granted until you have to provide it yourself."

"Me too," Fran said. She thirsted for the comfort that came with touch.

In a conversational tone, Mimi said, "Do you think maybe we should —"

"No." It might end their friendship, and right now Mimi was her only close friend.

"How do you know what I'm going to say?" Mimi's brown eyes darkened. "And why not?"

Not at all sure how she'd guessed, she laughed. "Not here. Okay? We'll talk later."

"I'm insulted," Mimi said as they circled Santa Land outside Dayton's.

Spying Sarah and Amelia coming out of the store, Fran stopped dead in her tracks. It was too late to flee. Amelia had seen her and, with a word to Sarah, veered toward her.

Fran willed her face blank, except for a slight tic near her right eye that she couldn't control. With a slight smile she acknowledged the scarlet sheen climbing Sarah's neck and suffusing her face.

Amelia asked, "How's the house, Fran?"

"I like it. My mother still thinks it's her old house, though. She's always looking for my dad and brother." It was true. Her mother got so agitated at times, she wondered if they'd have to move.

Sarah said, "Does it look so much like the house she used to live in?"

Fran studied Sarah for a brief moment. Did she care? "Yeah, it does. I never thought of her becoming disoriented by the familiar." Fran hoped the house wasn't hastening her mother's slide into confusion.

"How is she otherwise?" Sarah asked.

"Physically she's pretty good. Sometimes she doesn't know who I am, though." Her mother had told her that morning that she had a little girl named Fran too.

"I told her I'd come play cards sometime." Sarah's flush was fading.

"Come ahead. You might have to remind her how to play."

"Tell her I'll call," Sarah promised.

"I will," Fran said, sure that Sarah wouldn't. It was a polite game that hurt. She took Mimi's arm. "We should go. We've got lots of shopping to do." With a perverse pleasure, she watched Sarah's expression stiffen.

Once they were out of earshot, Mimi said, "You two sure create discomfort in each other."

Fran pretended a nonchalance. "Really?"

"You're sweating."

"It's warm in here with a jacket."

"Why don't you invite her over, Fran? This is foolish. You both care about each other."

"What makes you think that?"

"It's obvious."

"I'm not going to call her, Mimi," she said, surprised by sudden anger. "She's the one who left me."

"Stupid pride," Mimi muttered.

"It keeps me going. I don't want to talk about it. Let's look for something for my mother. What do you get a woman who needs so little?"

* * * * *

"Seeing her upsets you, doesn't it?" Amelia asked
as they walked away from Fran and Mimi.

"No." But she was damp from the encounter.

"You're a lousy liar, Sarah."

"Look, I don't want to feel this way." She didn't
understand her strong reaction to Fran. "It's a
physical thing." Her blood raced through her, pump-
ing color into her face, and she had no control over
it.

"It'll go away with time," Amelia said.

She hoped so. It was embarrassing to be so un-
done by the mere sight of one person.

Sarah went home to the comfort of her computer
that night. Joy had lent her *Writer's Market* at the
last writers' meeting. She was readying her story for
submission. However, the main character no longer
resembled Troy's mother. She had shown it to him
over the weekend, and he'd said, "It's good, cookie,
but it's not about my mother." Maybe that was
better.

All her adult life she had wanted to be a writer
but had never had the courage to follow through.
This gathering of would-be writers, by urging her to
submit her story to a magazine, lent her the confi-
dence she lacked.

Tapping out a letter to the editor of an obscure
magazine, she experienced a rush of excitement different from anything she'd previously known. As she

147

stuffed the story and letter into a manila envelope, she recalled her promise to call Fran's mother.

She asked for Rhea.

Fran sounded surprised. "I'll get her."

"Hello?" Fran's mother said, after what seemed a long time.

"Rhea, this is Sarah. How are you?"

"You must want Fran." The older woman's voice was thin, reedy.

"No. I called to talk to you." But it was too late. Rhea was summoning Fran back to the phone.

"Sarah, she probably wouldn't know who I am if *I* called. If you want to see her, it's better to tell me."

"I thought I'd come when you were gone, give you a break."

"I'll be out Thursday night."

"All right," Sarah said, caught in a web of her own making. Here she was trying to live up to her word. Did it take the good out of a deed to do it unwillingly?

"You're never home anymore, and when you are, you're holed up in your room," Troy complained when Sarah told him she would be gone Thursday, "leaving me stuck with Dale, who's behaving like an asshole."

"I noticed," she said dryly. He'd been sulking because Troy had invited her to spend Christmas with his parents. "Why don't you take him home with you. Amelia's giving me a hard time about it too. She thinks I should meet her folks."

"Is this getting serious?" His eyebrows hit his hairline.

"For her maybe. I wouldn't mind spending the day at her condo if she'd stay home."

"I'll think about it." He brightened. "The three of us could go."

"No, thanks." She had no wish to spend Christmas with Dale.

"Where're you going Thursday?" he asked. "To Amelia's?"

She told him, knowing he would read more into it than there was.

"Aha. You want to see Fran, don't you?" He sounded as if he'd uncovered some juicy piece of information.

"I'm following up on a stupid promise I made. Rhea doesn't even remember me."

"Want me to come with you?"

She was taken back. "Why would you want to?"

"I don't have anything else to do."

So Thursday evening she rang the doorbell at Fran's Cape Cod with Troy at her side. He made a great buffer, she thought. Light spilled out of the front windows onto the snow-covered yews beneath them and the yard beyond.

"Pretty, isn't it?" he remarked. "They're ice fishing on Lake Winnebago. We should go."

"We will, one of these weekends." Sitting on a bucket, watching tip-ups on the ice in the dead of winter was not one of her favorite pastimes.

Then a startled-looking Fran was framed in the open doorway. "Good to see you both. Mom's in the kitchen."

They were standing in a foyer with a small room

like a den to their left and a larger living room to their right. In front of them were the stairs to the second floor. They followed Fran down the hall past the staircase. Under it were a half-bath and beyond that a bedroom. A doorway opened from the hall to the dining room, and they went through a swinging door to the kitchen. Rhea looked up from loading the dishwasher.

"Mom, Sarah and Troy have come to spend the evening with you."

Rhea straightened, a dirty plate in one hand. "I know you, don't I?"

"Troy helped us move, and Sarah had dinner and played cards with you a few weeks ago," Fran said helpfully.

"Do you want some supper?" Rhea asked.

"No, thanks. We ate," Troy said.

"You beat the pants off me at spite and malice," Sarah said, hoping Rhea would remember something.

"Did I? Well, Franny's going to visit her girl-friend."

What the hell was she doing here, Sarah wondered, entertaining Fran's mother while she spent the evening with Mimi. Was she crazy? She gave Fran an angry look. "How is Mimi?"

"Good," Fran said with enthusiasm.

"Maybe she'd like to come over here," Troy suggested. "We could all play cards."

Sarah felt Fran's indecision.

Then Fran said, "We have other plans." She went to the back door and let in Butch, who greeted them with wild enthusiasm.

After Fran left, Sarah, Troy, and Rhea sat at the

kitchen table. Sarah had brought a deck of cards with her in case Rhea couldn't find one.

Troy was doing some fancy shuffling. "Want to play sheepshead?" he asked.

"Sure," Rhea said.

"You get first pick," he said to Rhea after dealing. She gathered the five cards in the middle and put them facedown on the table in front of her.

"Better look through them, Rhea, and keep the ones you want," Troy said with a glance at Sarah, "and discard five you don't want."

"Do you know how to play sheepshead, Rhea?" Sarah asked.

"Oh, yes," the older woman replied. "My husband taught me."

"You lead too," Troy prompted.

"So I do," Rhea said, leading a small trump.

Sarah put the ace of diamonds on the trick and Troy dropped the ten. Then she led an ace of hearts, Troy put on the ten, and Rhea dropped the ace of spades. Sarah and Troy looked at each other again. If Rhea had known how to play sheepshead, she had forgotten.

After that hand, they changed the game to hearts. Around eight-thirty Rhea excused herself and went to the bathroom. The dog padded after her. They heard the toilet flush, but she didn't return.

"I don't think she's coming back," Troy whispered at nine o'clock.

"I better make sure she's all right." Sarah went to the bathroom, which was open, then knocked on Rhea's closed bedroom door. When there was no answer, other than the dog shuffling on the other side, she turned the knob and looked in. Rhea was in bed, asleep. She could hear her breathing. Closing the door quietly, she returned to the kitchen.

Troy laughed all the way home. "We must be stimulating company. Here we are spending the evening with her, thinking we're doing her a favor, and she goes to bed in the middle of it."

"She probably forgot we were there," she said, struggling against feeling foolish.

Mimi wanted to eat at Hau's and go to the cheap movie theater down the street, where seats cost a dollar and seventy-five cents. *Apollo 13* was showing. Fran said nothing about Sarah and Troy spending the evening with her mother. She hoped playing cards wouldn't prove too frustrating for any of them. The last time she'd played spite and malice with her mother, she'd had to lead her through the game.

They ordered crabmeat rangoons, which Fran loved, and egg rolls and two glasses of wine. That would leave room for popcorn and Mason Dots at the theater. "You look tired, Mimi," she said. She hadn't seen her since their shopping trip earlier in the week.

"I am. Bob called five times last night. I'd just get to sleep and the phone would ring. Thanksgiving dinner gave him hope, I guess."

"Want to spend Christmas with me and Mom and Chelsey and maybe Chelsey's roommate, Jamie Lynn?"

"Thanks. I'll think about it." Mimi took a sip of wine, crossed her arms on the table, and looked at

Fran. "My attorney's going to file the divorce papers next week."

Fran put her glass down and met Mimi's dark gaze. "What do you think Bob will do?" Sure that he would react with anger, possibly violence, she was certain the rage would be directed at her as well as Mimi.

"I don't know. He's sort of unpredictable. He'll probably be furious."

"You could be in danger, Mimi." So could she herself, she thought.

"I know. I'll file a restraining order too."

XV

Sunday morning Troy called while Amelia and Sarah were still in bed.

Amelia answered, handing the phone to Sarah. "Troy wants to go ice fishing."

"It's a gorgeous day — sunny, not too cold," he said. "Come on, Sarah. You promised."

She wanted to write during the afternoon, but he'd spent that strange evening with her and Fran's mother. She owed him. "I'll be home after breakfast. Amelia has two open houses."

The Explorer bumped down a boat ramp onto Lake Winnebago. Following a makeshift road marked by tire tracks — approximately where they'd gone fishing the day of the storm — they headed toward several shanties that were clustered together with vehicles parked near them.

She was nervous about being out on the ice this early in the season, even though it was said to be ten inches thick already.

As if reading her thoughts, Troy said, "It's safe, cookie."

"Look at that crack." A long ridge of ice was pushed up at least a foot high and wide.

"The water wasn't frozen solid when that happened."

She wondered if the restless lake stopped stirring under its blanket of ice. They were driving over the sandbars so treacherous to boats. The depth was probably only a few feet.

Troy parked the Explorer so that it would act as a shelter against the raw wind sweeping out of the northwest across the flat expanse of frozen lake. She helped him pull the gasoline-powered ice auger out of the back of the truck. While he drilled holes in the ice, she got out the tip-ups and jigging rods, the minnows they'd bought for bait, the buckets they would sit on to jig. Then she scooped the ice out of the holes he'd made, measuring the depth of solidity against the dipper's long handle.

"There," he said, a little breathless but looking pleased with himself.

They baited the tip-ups, setting them so that the flags would pop up if anything tugged on the hooks.

After that, they put minnows on their jig rods and sat over a couple of holes in the ice, jerking the rods to attract fish.

"This is a great way to spend a Sunday afternoon, isn't it?"

"You wouldn't rather watch the Packers play?" she asked, wondering how many gay men were avid fishermen.

"Naw. I always wait for the play-offs. Besides, we can turn on the truck radio and listen to the game. Want to?"

"I don't care," she said indifferently, huddling deeper into her jacket. The cold seeped up from the ice into the soles of her boots. The sun was shining, but that meant whatever heat it produced escaped into the atmosphere. They could hear the sounds of the game coming from the ice shanties around them. She wanted the Packers to win, but she was interested in the results, not the play-by-play action.

"There goes a tip-up." Troy jumped from his bucket and ran to one of the holes. He pulled the line in by hand. A large perch hung on the end of it. "Want to keep it for supper tonight?"

She shook her head and watched him free the fish into the watery depths. Out of the corner of her eye, she saw another flag waving. "Tip-up," she yelled, rushing to it while he reset the hook on his. Grabbing the line, she hauled up a decent-size northern and held it for Troy to see. Then she released it.

By the time the sun dropped low in the sky, they had caught and released half a dozen perch and two northerns. When they stashed the gear in the back of the Explorer and climbed inside, she was chilled all the way through. Driving off the ice, she noticed the setting sun in the side mirror. It cast a mauve glow on the snow-blown surface behind them. She shivered. Nothing looked colder than the sun setting on an icebound lake.

Troy said, "You're the only person I know who likes to fish." He threw her a grin. "Did you see the size of the northern on my line?"

"Mine was just as big."

"We should have measured. What do you want to do for supper?"

"I suppose Dale will expect something to eat and us to fix it," she said.

"Let's surprise him and eat out."

"I don't know, Troy. I need to write something for Tuesday's writers' group."

"You can do it after we get home."

The Explorer climbed off the ice onto the snow-covered road. Warm air was beginning to blow out of the vents. She knew she wouldn't write tonight. Being outside for hours in the cold exhausted her. Yesterday she had put something together that she could polish tomorrow after work. It wouldn't make Amelia happy if she stayed home two nights in a row, but that was tough.

Troy parked at a bar across from the entrance to High Cliff State Park. "They used to have good hamburgers and french fries here. Want to try it?"

Inside, vapor rose off the pools of water on the floor and the clothes of the customers, most of whom wore snowmobile suits hanging down from their waists. The bar seats were taken, as were most of the high tables. One corner table was open, and they climbed onto the stools. They ordered Miller Lites, cheeseburgers, and fries.

"Hey, don't I know you?" A young guy with a crew cut and close-set eyes clumped over in his moon boots to their table.

Troy frowned. "I don't think so."

Sarah stared at the guy, trying to place him. From her vantage point, he looked like he should share the Packers' football bench. Her heart leaped into overtime.

"Sure I do. You were with that pansy who came into Eddie Bauer a few weeks ago."

"Not me," Troy said, looking truly bewildered. "This is my girlfriend, Sarah. We were ice fishing. How's the snowmobiling?" There had been at least eight of the machines parked outside.

"Bart," a girl called from the bar. "Food's here."

He stood before them, looking uncertain. "In a minute," he yelled to the girl, then spoke to Troy, "I was ready to punch your lights out." He shook Troy's hand. "The name's Bart," he said before lumbering back to the bar.

Troy sagged a little and whispered, "That was a close one."

It clicked. She remembered Dale and Troy coming out of Eddie Bauer laughing about Dale trying to pick up one of the salesclerks.

"Want to leave?" she asked.

"We've already ordered." He leaned over to confide in her, "I nearly shit in my pants. Did it show?"

"No," she replied. It hadn't. She'd thought she was the only one terrified.

When they were leaving the parking lot, cold air blowing on their legs, Troy said, "If I knew which snowmobile was his, I'd run it down. What a bully."

"Am I glad to be out of there." Her stomach hurt after nervously wolfing down the greasy food. She had hardly tasted it.

"What I ought to do is go home and beat up Dale." The Explorer spun its wheels, then caught the road's surface and jumped forward.

It had been a nightmarish three days. Thursday Bob had received the divorce papers. Livid with rage, he was waiting for Fran at work Friday morning. He waved them in her face when she punched in. No longer did she go inside for a cup of coffee.

"You done this to me. You talked her into it," he yelled.

Nina forced her way between them. "Cool down, Bob. It's time to run your route."

"I'm gonna get her and you for this," he said, trying to push aside Nina, who wouldn't budge.

"Thanks, Nina. Got to go. I'm sorry, Bob. I did my best." She jumped off the dock, nearly slipping on a patch of ice. Catching her balance, she hurried to her truck. Her ears roared with the sound of her fearful heart, her movement spurred by a rush of adrenaline.

Mimi had moved in with Fran Friday night. Now she wanted to stay. "He'll be waiting. I've got enough clothes for the week."

"He must know you're here," she said. But she didn't want to be alone either. They spent the weekend cooped up inside, only releasing Butch into the fenced-in backyard.

Whenever the phone rang, they looked at each other. Mimi had refused to answer her phone all week, only returning Fran's one-ring signals.

"Don't answer it," Mimi pleaded.

But it could be one of her kids, or Mimi's. She had to. This time it was Bob.

"You're running scared, aren't you?" he said. "You should be."

Grabbing the phone, Mimi yelled into the receiver, "Leave me alone." Then hung it up with a bang.

"What'd you do that for?" Fran asked, staring at Mimi as if she'd lost her mind. She glanced at her mother's door, but it remained shut. Her mother went to bed around eight these days.

"I'm going to call my sons," Mimi said, punching in a number.

"Bob's probably there."

"I have to take that chance." The receiver shook in Mimi's hand. "Bobby, this is Mom. I need your help." A pause followed. "That's the problem. Your father is threatening me. Can you talk to him?" Mimi chewed on her lip and listened. "I'm afraid, Bobby." She began crying. "Let me talk to Randy."

She had never seen Mimi cry, and she looked away, only turning back when Mimi hung up the phone. "What'd they say?"

"That their dad has a right to be angry, that I'm crazy to divorce him."

"What did they say when you told them you're afraid?"

"That their dad wouldn't hurt me." Mimi blew her nose and wiped her eyes, but the tears kept coming.

With sinking hopes, Fran stepped toward her friend. "Maybe they're right. Do you want me to come to court with you Monday?" A hearing on the restraining order was scheduled for Monday at one.

Looking like a person doomed, her eyes and nose reddened, Mimi nodded. "Can you?"

The courtroom was closed when Fran met Mimi and her attorney in the hallway the next afternoon. Bob was not there, nor was there another attorney.

"He doesn't have to be here," Mimi said.

"If he doesn't contest it, the restraining order will be automatically given," the attorney, a slightly overweight, middle-aged woman, attested.

The doors opened at one, and they went inside. Mimi and her attorney sat at a table on one side and in front of the bench. Fran took a seat on the pew-like bench behind the rail that separated the court from the audience. She turned when she heard the commotion in the hall.

"Wait, wait," Bob was saying, sailing down the aisle toward the judge. "I'm her husband. You can't keep me away from her. I have rights."

Behind him was hurrying a natty little man. "Your honor, I apologize," he said when he reached the defendant's table. He leaned toward Bob and hissed, "Sit down and be quiet."

The two young men who followed could only be Mimi's sons. One of them looked like her, one resembled Bob. Their size was intimidating.

Mimi paled and sat frozen in her chair, her gaze moving worriedly from her sons to her husband.

Fran was called on to testify. Looking at no one and in a quiet voice she told the judge about Bob's threatening behavior, his crashing into her home, his confrontations at work, his phone calls.

Mimi said that Bob had hit her one too many times, that she no longer believed him when he said he wouldn't harm her. She told the judge that she wanted him to stop harassing her and that she had filed for divorce.

Bob's sons spoke on their father's behalf, saying that he was despondent without their mother. When asked, neither admitted seeing their father strike their mother, but they didn't deny seeing the bruises. That was probably only when their mother asked for it, they said, acknowledging that they, too, hit their girlfriends once in a while, just to stop their nagging.

When Bob took the stand, he said he'd only been trying to save his wife from Fran, who was a dyke. He begged not to be kept from Mimi.

The judge granted the restraining order and told Bob to stay away from Mimi.

Wisely, Bob said nothing. He fixed an angry gaze on Mimi and Fran when they left the courtroom with Mimi's attorney.

Fran walked Mimi to her Blazer.

Mimi was crying. "They're chauvinists, my sons," she said. "They saw their dad hit me when they were little boys. They must have blocked it out, and now they're knocking their girlfriends around." She sobbed as she unlocked the Chevy. "I'm a failure, Fran."

"No, you're not," Fran assured her. "We'll talk about it tonight. Okay? We both have to get back to work."

Bob glared at them from across the street when they drove out of the courthouse parking lot. Maybe it was time to look for another job. She couldn't continue working with this man under these conditions.

When she parked the step-van at the dock that night, she punched the time clock and left. Once more she'd managed to avoid meeting Bob by hurrying through her route. On the way home, she decided to look through the Sunday classifieds.

Entering through the side door, she was surprised at how cold the house was. The furnace was running, yet there was a draft sweeping across the floors. Calling her mother's name, she walked through the rooms and found the front door open.

"Not today," she said involuntarily, then raised her voice. "Mom. Butch." No answer, no bark. She went through the rest of the house, knowing the dog and her mother were gone.

Getting back in the truck, she drove slowly through the streets. She found them in the park by the partially frozen river. Flinging the door open, she called, "Come on, Mom. Get in."

Her mother turned her head. She had no hat on, and her white hair blew like straw in the wind. Her face looked frozen, the lips blue, the nose and cheeks a burning red. The dog rushed toward the truck, dragging her mother behind him. When she fell, he continued his plunge toward warmth.

Jumping out of the Ranger, Fran raced toward her mother who looked up at her with bewildered eyes. "Mom, are you all right?"

"What are you doing here, Franny? I thought you were in school."

"Oh, Mom, why did you have to do this?" She lifted her mother to her feet and walked her to the truck. Butch greeted them with welcoming licks. "You worthless dog," she said, pushing him over to make room for her mother.

"We'll take the dog home, Mom. Then we'll eat and get your stuff together," she said, belting her mother in. "You're going to have to go back to Meadow Manor."

She was relieved now that she hadn't let go her mother's room at the assisted-living home.

Looking out the window at the snow skimming across the road in front of a brisk wind, Fran felt as bleak as the weather. Her mother sat with Mimi in the front of the Blazer.

"Where are we going, dear?" her mother asked.

She leaned forward and told her again, steeling herself against her own grief and any weakness that might cause her to change her mind.

The staff and elderly residents greeted them as the three of them walked to Fran's mother's room.

"What about Butch?" her mother asked while Fran unpacked her bags for her.

Close to tears, Fran ducked her head. Her voice betrayed her. "He'll be all right. I'll take care of him."

When Fran and Mimi left, her mother trailed after them to the door. She stood peering out the window as they got into the Chevy and drove off.

"She looks abandoned, Mimi," Fran said.

Mimi placed a comforting hand on her leg. "I know the feeling. My sons left me today."

"Oh, Mimi, I'm so sorry." She wrapped her fingers around her friend's hand.

"Don't cry," Mimi said. "Wait until we get home. I can't see to drive."

XVI

"You sure you don't want to come?" Troy asked, loading the Explorer with his and Dale's suitcases the Friday morning before Christmas. "Mom especially invited you."

Sarah had helped carry out the baggage, because Dale had a cold. "I know. Tell her hello." She'd decided she didn't need another mother, especially one who wasn't her own. "Do you think Dale's up to this trip?"

"I don't know, but he wants to go." He pulled his head and shoulders out of the back of the Ford.

"Brrr. Let's go inside, cookie. Have a cup of the black stuff together."

Dale was upstairs, showering. She poured herself and Troy the last of the coffee. "Look at the lines at the bird feeders," she said.

"I filled them this morning," he told her. "I'm counting on you to keep them that way. The little buggers have to eat."

"Of course." She enjoyed watching the birds as much as he did. Right now there were juncos and doves pecking at the ground and purple finches, goldfinches, a couple nuthatches, and two cardinals in the trees or on the feeders.

"Where are you going for Christmas? Have you decided yet?" he asked.

"I picked up a bunch of videos from the library. I'll hole up here and watch them."

"Wish I were doing it with you. And this weekend?"

"Amelia's leaving for her parents' on Saturday. She'll be here tonight."

"And Fran?" he asked.

"I don't know." She hadn't talked to Fran since the day after she and Troy had gone there to spend the evening with Rhea. Fran had laughed, too, when she'd told her that her mother had gone to bed in the middle of a game.

After Troy left with Dale, who was pale and red nosed, Sarah went up to her room and sat down in front of her computer. The library was closed through Christmas, giving her four vacation days.

She wrote to her mother:

This is my first Christmas without you,

Mom. I still miss you. Your death created a vacuum in my life that I didn't know how to fill. I left Fran a few months later. Maybe one led to the other. I don't know, but at the time I couldn't stay, wanting as I did to escape everything that was familiar.

She paused, her hands resting on the keyboard. Her mother had survived her father's death ten years earlier. What had that been like for her? Her mother hadn't run from her children or past memories. Sarah, on the other hand, had built a wall of grief between the present and the past.

Earlier in the week she'd bought a gift for Fran and her mother and put it in the mail — a detailed wood carving of a blue-winged teal to be used as a Christmas ornament. Perhaps Fran would call and thank her, and she would then tell her that she was sorry.

Suddenly she couldn't sit still and, clambering downstairs, browsed through the kitchen. Needing groceries for the meal that night, she pulled on her jacket and went out into the cold, snowy day.

At Copps, as she pushed her cart through the crowded aisles, she saw Candy and Georgie and wheeled over to where they were looking at the frozen turkeys. "Hey, you two, happy holidays."

"We hear you're going to be home by yourself," Georgie said. "You're more than welcome to spend Christmas with us."

"Thanks." She searched her brain for a polite refusal and found none. "I really need that time alone."

"If you change your mind, let us know," Candy said. "There's plenty of room at the table."

"I'll see you for sure at the next writers' meeting."

At home she turned on public radio and started dinner. Snow blanketed everything so that colored lights on trees and bushes and houses glowed inside the whiteness. Night had fallen when she finished shelling the shrimp for the fettuccine and went into the living room to strike a match to the pyramid of paper and kindling and oak she'd built behind the glass doors of the fireplace. Bringing in the newspaper, she sat for a few minutes to scan the front page and watch the fire catch.

Amelia arrived as she was setting the table for dinner. "Sell anything today?"

"I showed two guys empty buildings all afternoon. They're starting a computer service for people who can't understand the manuals." Amelia kissed her on the cheek. "Want some help?"

"Nope." She poured two glasses of cabernet sauvignon and lit the candles on the table.

"Nice. A romantic dinner," Amelia said.

"Our Christmas celebration."

"I wish you'd come with me."

They opened gifts in front of the fire after cleaning up the kitchen. Amelia gave her, among other things, a copy of the new *Writer's Market*.

"Remember me when you use it as a reference," she said, her smile wistful.

The next morning Amelia wakened her with touch. Cold light streamed through the frosted glass.

But Amelia's hand was warm as it caressed her, reaching beneath her undershirt and into her bikini undies. Sarah lay quietly for a few moments, letting desire gather, then rolled on top of Amelia to begin what was becoming, for her at least, a sexual routine.

Before going to the airport, Fran had picked her mother up from Meadow Manor, telling the staff that she would keep her through Christmas.

When Chelsey stepped from the Boeing 737 onto the portable staircase, Fran immediately recognized her. Her long hair wrapped thick curly tendrils around her face, and Chelsey gathered it behind her head with one hand. It always astonished Fran to see her daughter, who strode with such self-confidence toward the building. Chelsey was a younger, taller version of herself. Her hair was darker, her eyes a blue that was almost black, her shoulders broader. Sometimes, like now, she seemed larger than life.

"Mom," she exclaimed and wrapped Fran in a tight embrace. Then she took her grandmother gently into her arms.

"Hello, Jamie. Glad you could come," Fran said to the young woman who was shuffling her feet and grinning next to Chelsey. She gave her a hug, too. "This is Chelsey's grandma, Rhea."

Noticing the distress on Chelsey's face, Fran saw her mother as her daughter must: fragile and tiny, crumbling with age. "Shall we get your baggage?"

"We've got it on," Chelsey said, gesturing toward the large backpacks and book bags they each carried.

"You stay with Grandma. I'll get the truck."

When they reached the Cape Cod, Fran helped her mother out of the truck while the young women freed themselves from the small area behind the seats in the long cab. Chelsey took her grandma's arm. Fran unlocked the side door and turned on lights. Butch leaped at them, a small, black, furry ball dancing around their legs, whining deep in his throat.

"He is so cute," Jamie said, trying to pick him up. He resisted.

Chelsey bent to run a hand over him, but his interest was directed at her grandmother.

After depositing her grandma in a chair, Chelsey looked around. "Nice, Mom. It does look like Grandma and Grandpa's old house."

"I'll show you to your room, and then we can have a little snack or something. I suppose they fed you on the plane?"

They went upstairs. Butch was in a quandary over whon to follow. He chased up the steps with them, then raced downstairs. After leaving the girls, and she still thought of them as girls, Fran went looking for her mother and found her in her room behind the stairs.

"Your grandmother's gone to bed," she told Chelsey in the kitchen where she put water on to heat for hot chocolate.

"Grandma looks at least ten years older than when I last saw her. She didn't say more than five words on the way home."

"I know," Fran said. It was as if her mother couldn't hold a thought long enough to express it. "I had to take her back to Meadow Manor. Among other

171

things, she wandered off. But I think she'll be all right this weekend with all of us here. She may cramp our style, because we can't go off without her."

"We'll take her with us," Chelsey said.

Shyly, Fran studied her daughter and Jamie over the kitchen table. Jamie was shorter and heavier than Chelsey. She had large gray eyes, an expressive face, and a contagious smile. She wore what Fran thought was a typical lesbian haircut: a perm, long in the back, short on the sides and top.

"We're having company for Christmas eve and day. A friend of mine." She told them as much as she thought she should about Mimi's difficulties.

"Some man shot his wife and himself the other day. She was divorcing him. They both died," Chelsey said. "This guy might hold you responsible, Mom."

"She's straight," she said, knowing he blamed her anyway.

"Are we going to have to pretend?" Chelsey asked, looking immediately annoyed.

"No. Mimi knows. She doesn't care."

"Do you ever see Sarah anymore, Mom? I just got used to her and you broke up."

"Once in a while I run into her." She changed the subject. "What do you want to do while you're here?"

"See some people. Drive around and look at things. This is still home." She gave Jamie an inclusive smile.

"Is it?" Fran asked, surprised.

"Mom, wherever you are is home."

Fran was inordinately pleased. It was the most affirming statement her daughter had made to her

172

since she was a child. If it was the only present she received this year, it would do. She'd carry it with her to keep her warm.

Saturday's mail brought Sarah's gift, addressed to her and her mother. Chelsey and Jamie had taken the truck and gone to the store. Fran carried the box into the living room and opened it in front of her mother. She turned it over in her hands, admiring its intricacy. She hung it on the tree.

Sarah answered the phone. "So you got it. I wondered."

"Today," she said. "Thank you." She hadn't bought anything for Sarah. "It's lovely. Makes me think of being up north."

"That's what I thought of when I saw it." There was noise in the background.

"I won't keep you. Sounds like you have company."

"That's a video. I'm all alone as a matter of fact," Sarah said.

"Where are your friends?" That sounded stupid. She knew their names. "Troy and Amelia and Dale."

"They've gone to their respective family homes."

"Would you like to come for Christmas dinner?" she asked.

"What I want to say, Fran, is that I'm sorry."

"So am I," she said, not exactly sure what they were referring to. Being sorry didn't change anything, though.

"I'll let you know about dinner. Merry Christmas anyway."

* * * * *

Christmas day dawned cold and clear. Mimi had spent the night, sleeping on the futon in the small upstairs bedroom Fran used as an office. Her hair was wet from showering and she was in the kitchen making coffee when Fran shuffled into the room.

"You're up early."

"I didn't sleep well. Every time I heard a car or truck go by I thought it was Bob coming to get me. By the way, merry Christmas."

"Same to you." Fran went into the living room to turn on the tree lights and start a fire.

Mimi brought her a cup of coffee and set it on the hearth. "I think I should go home. I've got a bad feeling about today."

Fran was kneeling in front of the fireplace wadding newspaper into balls and stuffing them under the grate. "You can't let hunches make your decisions, Mimi. Nothing's going to happen today. You said Bob and your sons were going to spend Christmas at your parents'."

"Doesn't that suck? I'm the outcast, their daughter. They took his side, knowing that he knocks me around." Mimi sat on the sofa.

Leaning back on her heels, she looked at Mimi. She was lovely, even with wet, stringy hair. Too bad she was straight. "Don't leave. I'd miss you."

"You're the best friend I ever had, Fran. Do you know that?"

Another confirmation. In addition to being appreciated as a mother, Mimi thought she was a wonderful friend. Maybe Sarah would show up and say she'd been an excellent lover. Smiling to herself, she turned back to the fireplace. "We've seen each other through some difficult times, haven't we?"

174

"I think you make a better friend than a hetero-sexual woman."

She laughed and struck a match to the paper. "That's an interesting observation." Picking up her coffee cup, she sat in the ancient easy chair that had belonged to her parents. The fire briefly roared, then settled into a crackling sound as the wood began to burn.

Carrying a cup of coffee, Chelsey joined them in the living room. The three of them stared at the flames.

"I better let the dog out," Fran said, getting up and quietly opening her mother's door.

Butch emerged, his tail whipping his small body back and forth. Letting him out into the backyard, she waited with arms crossed behind the storm door. He nosed through mounds of snow, searching for the right spot to make his deposit. His head jerking upright and his sudden, unexpected bark were the only warnings she had.

Bob stood before her, filling the door frame. He looked huge, menacing. "Where is she?"

Bewildered by his unexpected appearance, she stared at him stupidly. "What are you doing here?" She saw the gun, just before he backhanded her with it.

He thrust past her as she slowly slid down the open door. The side of her face was numb. Putting a hand to it, she felt a thick, gooey wetness. It's crushed, she thought, looking toward the living room where there was shouting. Outside, she heard Butch barking.

"Mimi, run."

Struggling to her feet, she took a few steps toward the pandemonium in the other room. Her head spun and nausea flooded her throat. She grabbed the table. Through a persistent ringing, she heard Chelsey and knew her daughter was holding her up.

"Mom, Mom. Oh god, oh god." Then Chelsey hollered in her ear, "Jamie, come down here."

A cold wind was coursing around her bare ankles. Someone should close the back door, get the dog inside. Then she felt his little tongue on her face and realized she must be lying on the floor. The shouting had stopped. She strained to hear Mimi's voice.

"Call 911, Jamie," Chelsey said, kneeling over Fran.

"Is Mimi all right?" Fran whispered.

"What the hell happened?" Jamie said.

"Don't leave your grandma alone, Chelsey."

She heard sirens. Chelsey and Jamie had helped her to the couch. She knew now that Bob had taken Mimi at gunpoint out the front door and forced her into his car. The son of a bitch had been crying, Chelsey said as she assured Fran that the police were already in pursuit.

Insisting on talking to the attending police before the emergency medical technicians hauled her off to St. Elizabeth's, she told two officers about the restraining order, about Bob's violent behavior. "Don't let him kill her," she begged, battling a peculiar sense of fate, an awareness of events spiraling out of control — as if whatever happened was already ordained.

"I'll follow in the truck, Mom," Chelsey said as

176

they loaded her onto a gurney. "Jamie will stay with Grandma."

"Where is your grandma anyway?" Maybe in all the turmoil she had wandered off.

"She's getting dressed, Mom."

At the hospital X rays were taken before a doctor numbed the wound with anesthetic. That was the worst part, the needle poking around in the raw flesh. "What happened?" he asked, as he cleaned and stitched the broken skin together.

She closed her eyes. "You tell him, Chelse," she said, using her daughter's childhood nickname. The hopelessness of the situation and her own helplessness tired her.

Chelsey spoke from where she sat in a chair against the wall near the door. Her voice was flat.

The doctor told Fran, "You're lucky there are no broken facial bones. A blow to the face like that can inflict terrible damage."

She found herself fighting sleep. The side of her face was without feeling, and she wondered what she looked like. Recalling the morning, she berated herself for being so naive. Belatedly, she realized that Mimi had known the inevitability of what had happened. There was no prevention, no cure. He would have gotten to Mimi sooner or later, no matter what they did.

XVII

Late morning, after Troy phoned, Sarah called Fran. She was suddenly so lonely she was willing to take her up on her invitation — unless Mimi answered the phone. Then she would do nothing more than extend Christmas wishes. She didn't recognize the answering voice, and when she asked for Fran, the girl said, "Fran's at the hospital." She sounded young.

"Chelsey?" she asked.

"No, I'm Jamie. Chelsey and I are visiting. Something terrible happened."

"To Fran's mother?" The alarm in the girl's voice frightened her.

"No, she's all right. Mimi was dragged off by her husband."

"What?" She didn't know Mimi had a husband, but then she'd never asked. "I'm coming over."

Five minutes later, she was parking outside the Cape Cod. When she walked toward the door, a policewoman from a squad car parked across the street approached and asked her her business there. It was then she knew that something awful had really taken place. Her body responded, her heart clamoring as adrenaline sped through her system. Apparently satisfied with her answer, the woman let her ring the bell.

The young woman who opened the door looked at her with mistrustful, scared eyes. "Are you Sarah?"

Rhea was sitting in the old chair in the living room with the dog at her feet. He wagged his body at Sarah. "Are we going to open presents now?" Rhea asked, her lined face lit by the sunlight that flooded the room.

"When Fran gets home," Sarah said.

"We always eat breakfast first," Rhea told her.

"Jamie and I'll fix something." In the kitchen she asked Jamie what had happened.

The words spilled out of the younger woman, filling Sarah with bleak surprise. How could all this happen without her knowledge?

"Fran's face?"

"It was so covered with blood, I couldn't tell." Jamie shuddered. "God, I'm glad you're here. It's like a nightmare without an end. Some Christmas."

Rhea stood in the doorway, looking from one to

the other. "What's your name, honey?" she asked Jamie.

"She keeps asking me who I am," the girl muttered, before saying loudly, "I'm Jamie, Chelsey's friend."

"Don't wake her. She needs her sleep."

"She's not in bed," Jamie said.

"She's at the hospital with Fran," Sarah explained, knowing she couldn't leave these two and go there as she wanted to.

"Franny was a good mother. She doesn't deserve this," Rhea said, making her way to a kitchen chair.

Sarah set two bowls of oatmeal on the table and buttered the toast. She'd already had her breakfast. "Eat, you two," she said.

Butch sat at Rhea's side, watching the food disappear into her mouth, gobbling the crusts she tore off for him. "He has to eat too," she said. After breakfast, she disappeared into her room.

It occurred to Sarah that one day Rhea would probably go to sleep and not wake up. There were worse ways to die. "I think I'll call the hospital," she said.

A woman in ER told her that Fran had been treated and released.

Fran's face was cleaned and stitched. She had seen it and knew it looked dreadful, swollen and bruised, but she felt nothing. She had filled the prescriptions for antibiotics and pain relievers at the hospital pharmacy. Nothing else would be open today.

While Chelsey parked in the garage, she talked to the police watching over them from the squad car out front. They told her Bob was holding Mimi hostage at their house. She wanted to go there and share Mimi's terror. It was the least she could do as a friend.

"Stay away," the woman officer said, as if reading her mind. "He's aggravated enough."

"Why don't you go home. It's Christmas." Maybe she could slip away. "We'll be fine."

"Give us some coffee instead," the other officer, a younger man, said.

"Come inside and warm up." At least she'd keep abreast of things that way.

"Thanks, but we have to stay out here until we're relieved."

While they'd talked, the police radio had sputtered out a running commentary. The neighbors' homes had been vacated. No sign of Bob or Mimi inside the house, but Bob's car was parked outside. Bob and Mimi's sons were on their way over.

"Come on, Mom. You need to go inside." Chelsey was tugging on her sleeve.

Realizing that her daughter was right, that she needed to lie down, she walked with her to the front door. As she turned the latch, Sarah pulled the door open.

"What are you doing here?" she asked in total surprise.

"You invited me to dinner. Looks like I'm going to have to make it."

"Boy, is it ever good to see you, Sarah." Chelsey led Fran to the couch.

"Where's Mom?" Fran asked, seeing Jamie's pale face. Poor girl. What a way to spend Christmas vacation.

"In bed," Sarah said. "Would you like something to eat?"

"Toast, please." The dog was standing with his front feet in her lap. She remembered his tongue on her face and ran a soothing hand over his soft hair. "I'm fine, Butch."

"Those cops want coffee," Chelsey said.

"I'll make some, and then we'll start dinner," Sarah said. "I know. Nobody's hungry right now, but it'll give us something to do."

Fran lay on the couch, unwilling to go to her bed. She'd taken a pain pill at the hospital and was staving off sleep with thoughts of Mimi. How could she close her eyes when Mimi's life was in danger?

Unable to absorb the enormity of Mimi's dilemma, Sarah saw it through Fran's wound — the discoloration, the incipient swelling, the stitches threading through the damaged flesh — and tried to fend off her helplessness with action. She'd made the coffee and was now going through the fridge and cupboards grabbing the makings for Christmas dinner.

"Pie first," she said to Chelsey and Jamie. "Follow the recipe on the pumpkin can."

She cut up three loaves of bread to make stuffing. This she could comprehend, the dicing of onions and celery, not the heedless destruction of lives. Yet here was a turkey, neatly plucked and ready to stuff, that had been butchered for her eating enjoyment. Maybe

Bob thought no more of taking his wife's life than he would of shooting a turkey.

When the stuffing was done, the smell of it making her stomach cramp in hungry anticipation, she crammed it into the turkey and with Chelsey's help put the bird in the oven. Then she peeled sweet potatoes, sending the peelings flying furiously, and set them in a water-filled pan to await boiling. Chelsey placed a hand on Sarah's sleeve.

"What?" she asked, startled by the touch.

"Mom's going to be all right," Chelsey said.

Was the girl looking for reassurance or giving it? Turning off the burner, she gave Fran's daughter a hug.

Chelsey burst into tears.

"I know, I know," Sarah said, patting the girl's back and wondering what it was she knew, if anything at all. She heard Fran's mother in the other room.

"Franny, you fell off your bike again."

"Don't I wish," Fran said.

Day turned into evening. The aroma of roasted turkey saturated the air. Plates of food were taken to the police in the squad car, and in the house they sat down to eat. Only Fran's mother cleaned her plate. Fran picked at her food, taking tiny bites which she chewed into pulp and forced down her throat. Voices from the TV and radio droned in the background. The evening news showed pictures of Mimi and Bob and the house where they had lived so many years and where he now held her hostage.

Fran put down her fork and knife and met Sarah's eyes. "I have to go there," she said quietly.

"I'll take you," Sarah replied.

"But the cops said it would only agitate him," Chelsey protested.

"I'll stay out of sight."

They took Sarah's truck. The squad car followed. Fran directed Sarah to the barricaded street, which was jammed with two fire trucks, two rescue wagons, and four police cars. It was filled with light and sound just as it had been on television. Outside the barred area were TV trucks and more police cars.

Sarah looked at her. "Do you want to get out?"

"Yes." She was shaking. It had been close to ten hours since Mimi had been hauled off. She wanted to see her, to tell her to hang on.

One of the cops that had been tailing them approached Sarah's truck and tapped on the window. "Go home," he said. "You can't do any good here."

"I want to know if she's all right." Cold air blew inside as she pleaded.

"We'll keep you informed."

"Can't we just wait here and watch? He can't see us."

"All right, for a while. Don't leave your vehicle," he ordered.

They heard one of Mimi's sons pleading through the megaphone. "Come on, Dad. Let Mom go. Everything will be all right."

It was a lie. She knew Bob wouldn't be fooled by false promises.

Sarah said, "You're shivering, Fran. You shouldn't be out here."

"I have to be, Sarah. I'm the best friend she ever

had, she told me that. I want to be able to tell her I was here."

"Then wrap this around you." Sarah fished behind the seat and pulled out an old wool blanket.

She recognized it. "This has a long history." They had sat on it during picnics and lain on its rough surface when making love outdoors and covered themselves with it after skiing while the truck warmed up. But even encased in the blanket, she shook.

"Tell me about Mimi," Sarah said.

"Remember Bob, the guy I work with?" She told Sarah how his asking for her help had led to her friendship with Mimi. "I realized this morning in ER that nothing could have saved Mimi from Bob. A restraining order wasn't going to keep him away. Instead it aggravated him, like a slap on the hand. He only understands violence. You'd have to shoot him to keep Mimi safe."

Sarah said, "It happens every day."

Snuggling into the blanket, Fran warmed herself enough to fall asleep. She incorporated the first shot into her dream, where, knowing that the bullet was aimed at herself and realizing that she couldn't run fast enough, she ran anyway. Her feet were heavy with her hopelessness, yet she was desperate with fear.

At the slew of shots that followed, she jerked upright, remembering where she was and what was going on. Shrugging off the blanket, she stepped outside. The shock of breathing the bitterly cold air sloughed off the dregs of sleep.

When she reached the barricade, Sarah forced Fran into a crouch behind the nearest police car. "Down."

Moments after it erupted, the barrage of gunfire ceased. Shouting followed, and Sarah's grip loosened. They stood and looked over the top of the black-and-white car with its bubble light. Cops were running toward the house.

"We'll wait here," Sarah said, tightening her hold.

They were carrying someone out of the house on a gurney. Fran broke loose and stumbled toward the rescue wagon as the EMTs loaded whoever it was into the ambulance. But Sarah caught up with her.

"Come on," Sarah said. "Get in the truck. We'll follow."

The ambulance was easy to keep track of, escorted as it was by police cars with their blue-and-red lights turning and sirens blaring. Parking in the hospital lot, they walked into the emergency room where she had been treated that morning. It was twelve-thirty according to the clock on the wall. Christmas was over. The room spun, and she sat with a thump in the nearest chair.

Mimi had been shot but was in stable condition. Sarah got this much information from the woman behind the admitting desk, who looked at Fran and asked if she needed immediate attention.

Sarah answered, "She needs to go home."

Mimi's sons pushed through the doors. They glanced at her without recognition. But Fran knew them from the day in court when they had testified in favor of their father. They were accompanied by two policemen and asked to see their mother.

Outside, her face ached in the frigid night. Funny, she hadn't noticed the pain earlier. Every muscle hurt as she climbed slowly into the truck. She rewrapped herself in the blanket. When Sarah turned the key, the radio came on with the news:

"The standoff is over. Robert Dombrowski — who broke into a residence early yesterday morning, kidnapped his estranged wife at gunpoint, and held her hostage in their home until police stormed the building after hearing a shot fired — is dead, killed by a sharpshooter at midnight. Mimi Dombrowski was hospitalized in stable condition after being shot in the side while trying to escape."

Her own tears startled her, and she wondered whether she wept from relief or sadness or exhaustion. Bob, having first wounded Mimi, had been shot dead and she was glad of it.

Sarah reached across the cab and took her hand.

Thousands of stars littered the sky. They drove past buildings and trees and bushes adorned with Christmas lights. Santas perched on housetops with their trusty sleighs and reindeer nearby. Manger scenes rested on snow-covered lawns, and hanging from lampposts were angels made from gold-colored garlands.

XVIII

The next morning on the way to the airport, Fran took her mother back to Meadow Manor. Chelsey said good-bye to her grandmother, who watched, as before, from the front windows. Fran cried as she started the truck and drove away.

"Mom, are you sure you're all right?" Chelsey asked, placing a hand on Fran's leg.

"I'm fine," she lied, then added with a shaky smile, "We're going to remember this as the Christmas from hell."

"Maybe you should visit us next year. We'll

arrange to have the building burn down." Chelsey glanced at her. "Just kidding, Mom. I hate leaving you like this."

"We never even opened presents," she suddenly wailed. Appalled with herself, she saw her daughter exchange an alarmed look with Jamie.

"I can stay a few days longer," Chelsey said.

Forcing a calm firmness into her voice, she stopped crying. "No, Chelse. What good would that do? It won't change anything. I'm okay, really."

She watched the plane taxi to the runway before leaving. People stared at her face. Some even asked how she hurt herself. Had she been in an auto accident, had she neglected to wear a seat belt, was the car totaled. "No," she said to the questions.

From the parking lot she raised her face skyward as the plane circled toward the southeast, heading for Chicago. Tears flowed down her cheeks, burning the stitches, blurring her vision.

She drove to work, where Nina was waiting.

"Go home," Nina said. "Boss's orders. All deliveries canceled today."

Dismayed to find herself in tears once more, she nodded.

"I called. You'd already left. Is there anything I can do?"

Fran was sobbing now.

"I'll follow you home. Okay?"

Nina took the key from her as Fran fumbled with the lock. The dog was barking frantically. Before yesterday he'd only looked at the door with quiet interest when someone was on the other side trying to get in.

"I'll fix us a cup of coffee," Nina said.

Fran gathered Butch in her arms and buried her face in his struggling body. "It's you and me now." The words caused her to begin crying again, and he licked her face before jumping to the floor.

Nina stood by the coffee pot, watching her. "Is there anyone I can call?"

Shaking her head, Fran took a deep breath that ended in a sob. "I think I'll lie down." She wandered into the living room, saw the unopened presents under the tree, and began crying again.

When she awakened, Sarah was sitting in the easy chair reading a book. "Nina called."

"Will you go with me to visit Mimi?" Fran grimaced, the stitches tearing at the fabric of her skin as if the wound had shrunk during sleep.

"Sure."

"I'll call her first."

When she came on the line Mimi said, almost as if nothing had happened, "I wondered when I'd hear from you. They told me you were here last night. When I last saw you, you were stretched out on the floor. Are you okay?"

"Better than you are, I'm sure."

"I want to see for myself."

Mimi resembled a wax figure, her skin pale and lustrous against the snow-white sheets. A light sheen of sweat beaded her face. Her smile looked painful, her lips nearly colorless. "Does it hurt?"

Fran shook her head. "Not much. How about you?"

"It feels like a stitch in my side. It's difficult to breathe. I lost a lot of blood."

Sarah was waiting downstairs because Mimi's visitors were limited to Fran, whom she'd asked for, and her sons and parents. "I don't want to see any of them. They blame me, I know they do. It makes me angry."

Better than crying all the time as she had been doing. "How are you otherwise?"

"The psychologist came to see me just before you got here, asking stuff like that," Mimi said. The pupils in her eyes nearly blotted out the color. Her voice was flat. "Bob's dead."

"I know. It all seems unreal."

"He jerked and jerked. Do you think it hurt much?" Tears spilled down Mimi's face.

"I don't know, Mimi," Fran said, weeping with her. "Have you cried a lot?"

Mimi shook her head. "I just wanted him to leave me alone. I didn't want him dead."

"He wasn't going to let you go," she said.

"Why?"

She stood and gently wiped the wetness off Mimi's face. "It wasn't in him. He thought you belonged to him."

Mimi took a deep breath that ended in a whimper. "I know."

Sarah called Troy from the hospital waiting room.

"I've been trying to get hold of you all day," he said. "Did you hear what happened?"

"I was there." She gave him a rundown of Christmas day and night.

He absorbed it silently. "Did you come home last night?"

"This morning I did. I caught a couple hours sleep at Fran's last night, then went home and took a shower and left for work. You were already gone, and Dale must have been asleep. How is he anyway?"

"Better. Actually, we had a surprisingly good time. Are you coming home tonight?"

"I don't know. It depends on Fran. She can't stop crying. I'm at the hospital with her right now."

"There was a message from Amelia on the machine last night," he said.

"I have to call her."

She was paging through a *People* magazine when Fran found her. "How was Mimi?"

"Hard to tell. She's going to stay with me when she gets out, at least for a while."

"Does she have family?"

"Her sons, her parents. They blame her for what happened," Fran said.

"It's good that she has you to stay with then."

"I don't want to be alone right now. I dread going home. Will you stay the night?"

Sarah shot a glance at Fran in the glare of the day. The side of her face was a nasty sight.

"Just one night, Sarah. Is that too much to ask?"

"I'll swing by my place and get some stuff."

While Fran waited in the truck, Sarah went inside to grab some clothes and pack her overnight bag. She called Amelia's real estate office and left a message on her voice mail. Dale was in the den. She heard the TV but couldn't bring herself to say hello.

* * * * *

In the bedroom Chelsey and Jamie had shared, Sarah lay listening to Fran sob. She knew that uncontrollable crying was a result of depression, but she didn't know what to do about it.

Amelia had called earlier in the evening. "When are you going home?" she'd asked.

Since Fran was lying on the couch, Sarah had to phrase her sentences with care. "You heard what happened?"

"Yes. Troy told me. I'd hoped to spend the night with you."

"Maybe tomorrow."

"We'll talk then," Amelia had replied, clearly annoyed.

The windows in the room were frosted over and radiated cold. She got up and padded down the hall. "Are you all right, Fran?" Peering into the room, she made out the double bed with its massive headboard.

Fran said, "I don't know what's wrong with me."

Sarah stepped into the room. "You need to talk to someone who can help you. I'm not that person."

"Why did he have to do such a stupid, asshole thing?"

Slipping under the covers, Sarah wrapped Fran in her arms in a last-ditch attempt to stop the tears. Aware of Fran's scent, her soft breasts and belly, her smooth skin, she said, "I don't know. You should try to sleep now. Things always look better in the morning." She could feel Fran's heart beating, her chest heaving.

"How's she going to get over this, Sarah?"

"I don't know, Fran. I should go back to my own

193

bed." But she was sleepy, and Fran's body comforted her. She let herself dream.

After work the next day, Fran made a quick trip home to take care of the dog, then drove to the hospital. She'd promised Mimi she would visit that night. When she reached her door, she heard voices inside and paused. She had no wish to come face-to-face with Mimi's parents or her sons, but she couldn't allow their presence to drive her away either. She knocked and entered.

Mimi had a roommate, whose visitors were making the noise. They nodded and said hello to her with interest.

"I thought you had company," she said.

Color had returned to Mimi's face. "They're at the funeral home. Bob's funeral is tomorrow."

"I don't think I'll go."

"Me, either," Mimi said. "I won't be discharged until Friday. My family thinks I should go to the funeral anyway."

"Do you want to?" They were whispering.

"No. I want to blot the past few days from my mind."

Fran gestured with her head at the people gathered around the other bed. "Do they know?"

"They act like they do. I feel like a bug under a microscope."

"Do you need anything from your apartment?"

"We'll get it over the weekend." Mimi looked at her beseechingly. "I'm sorry he hurt you."

"I'm sorry about the whole thing," Fran said, digging her nails into her palms. So far today, she had fought off tears.

When she left, she couldn't bear to go home alone after dark. Even though she knew Bob was dead, part of her believed he was waiting for her. A vestige of terror hung over the house. Finally, after driving for an hour through cheerfully decorated neighborhoods, she parked in the garage and hurried to the side door. She had left lights on inside, and the dog was waiting to welcome her.

The red light flashed on her machine. It was Sarah, checking up on her. She phoned.

"She's not here," Troy told her. "How are you doing after that dreadful ordeal? What a nightmare."

"Yes. I was afraid to come home. Silly, huh, as if he'd be lurking in the bushes."

"Not at all. I'd be scared witless. Let me come over and keep you company."

"Thanks, Troy, but I'm okay now that I'm inside with the doors locked. The dog is here." He was sitting on her feet, pushing his head against her hand, looking for a rub.

"How's Mimi?"

"She'll be discharged Friday if her blood count is high enough. She's going to stay with me for a while." That would be a comfort. "Tell Sarah I returned her call, will you? Nice of her to be concerned."

"She loves you," Troy said.

The pause between them was the length of three heartbeats. "Sure. That's why she's with Amelia," she said. "Actually, though, she prefers your company, or so she says. I'm not much fun these days." She didn't want to sound bitter and quickly added, "Sorry."

"Me too, Fran. Life can be a bastard."

"Something wrong?"

"Let me come over and tell you."

"Not tonight," she said.

"Tomorrow then. I'll fix you dinner."

"I can't. I have to visit both my mother and Mimi tomorrow night."

They decided, instead, that he would go with her to bring Mimi home from the hospital.

If the bathroom hadn't been down the hall, she would have propped a chair under her door when she went to bed. Instead, she left the hall light on and kept the dog close by.

For dinner Amelia had made chicken fajitas, Spanish rice, and refried beans. After eating, they cleaned up the mess and took their wine to the living room where the gas fire burned behind glass doors.

"We need to talk," Amelia began, her smoky eyes light from the fire. She patted the couch next to her.

Sarah sat, facing her. She was nervous, not knowing what Amelia would say, unsure how she would reply. "What?"

"You spent last night with Fran. I have to know how you feel about her."

"She didn't want to be alone. You know what happened."

"Why were you there in the first place?"

"I took her to see Mimi."

"Did you spend Christmas with her too?"

Sarah heaved a sigh. Her back was against the proverbial wall. She could continue to be evasive or try to figure out the truth. "I don't know how I feel about either one of you."

Amelia took a deep breath and expelled it. "When are you going to know?"

"Look, Amelia, you said we didn't have to be serious, that we could just have fun."

"When we got into bed together, it became serious," Amelia said. "But you're right. I did say that. It's just that I don't think you've given us much of a chance."

"I'm not ready for another relationship," she said.

"You're not over Fran. I don't know why you left her. Whenever you see her, it's obvious."

"How?"

"You both get flustered. Maybe she's not over you either."

Sarah set her glass of wine on the coffee table. It added color to the room. "Do you want me to stay or not?"

"No, I don't think so. Give me a little time, Sarah. Maybe we can be friends."

Outside, Sarah's breath puffed white in the night. With each stride her steps lightened until she was nearly running. She wanted to walk home, but her truck was parked down the street. First, though, she drove around, listening to *Messiah* and looking at the brightly lit homes and yards. She was free. It made her want to shout. Instead, she sang along with the tape.

When she reached Troy's house, it was dark. But once she was in her room, he knocked on the door.

"Well, cookie, what are you doing home?" He was wrapped in his chenille robe.

"My mother had bedspreads like that," she said, a big grin on her face.

"I think it's chic," he said. "Why do you look like the Cheshire cat?"

"Amelia asked me to leave." Multicolored fish swam across her monitor, and an urge to write seized her.

"It's over then? You and Amelia?" She nodded and he continued, "I'm not surprised."

She touched the mouse, and words replaced the swimming fish.

"Fran called tonight. She's afraid that what's-his-name will jump out at her. I offered to go over, but she said she was all right. I'm going with her to get Mimi from the hospital Friday."

Maybe she would go too. "I'll call her tomorrow," Sarah said, her grin gone. It was too late tonight. She should have driven over to check on her after she left Amelia. "How's Dale?"

"He's pretty much recovered from his cold. My mother clucked over him all weekend. He ate it up."

XIX

Although safely ensconced in the spare bedroom, Mimi's presence wasn't making Fran feel secure. Mimi woke screaming in the night, causing Fran to rush to her side with Butch at her heels. Sitting on the edge of Mimi's bed Sunday night, she wondered what to do.

"I'm so sorry, Fran." Mimi was panting. "I see him in the doorway, dragging himself toward me, and he's terribly wounded — like the son in *The Monkey's Paw*, remember that? — and he's blaming me."

"You need help, Mimi. That psychologist at the hospital, why don't you give him a call tomorrow?"

"I will." Mimi looked small and frightened, huddled in the far corner of the bed.

"I'll sleep with you. Will that help?"

"Yes, oh yes. Please."

As Mimi's breathing evened out, Fran lay awake. They were a matched pair, two frightened women. Finally exhaustion claimed her, and she curled into a ball and slept.

Fran had invited Sarah, Troy, and Brad for cards Saturday evening. Saturday morning she went to Meadow Manor to bring her mother home for the weekend. With Mimi so weak she had seen little of anyone else.

"This is my daughter, Franny," her mother said to one of the staff.

"Are you all right, Fran?" the woman asked. They were in the sunlit living room. "We were so worried."

"Thanks. I'm okay." The side of her face was now a mustardy brown.

"You hurt yourself," her mother said, gently touching the wounded cheek.

"And the woman who was held hostage? How is she?" The other staff member on duty had joined them.

"Mimi. She's all right physically. It's not an easy thing to get over."

"Mimi," her mother said as if trying to place the

name. "I know a Mimi. Your friend with the blue car."

"Yeah, Mom. That's her. She's home, waiting for us."

"What is it, Troy?" Sarah asked Saturday morning as she watched him throw pans into the lower cupboard.

"There's not room for all this shit," he said.

"Yes, there is." Taking a dutch oven out of his grasp, she made a place for it. "You have to be patient is all. Why do you have to be in a foul mood, when I'm in such a good one?"

"I don't know how to tell you what he did. You won't believe it." He stood in bare feet and sweats, his hair pointing in all directions.

"Try me," she said, running her fingers through her hair. "You might be surprised."

"You know how worried I've been, how angry I was because I knew he cheated." He stomped over to the table and sat down in front of his cup of coffee.

"We are talking about Dale, right? Is he going with us tonight?" She hoped to sidetrack his anger.

"He has to work, which is just fine with me." He took a swig of coffee. "Do you want to hear this or not?"

"Of course, I do. Where is he anyway? In bed?"

"Asleep. I should smother him now." The sun shone on his face, and she was reminded of last summer. "He isn't HIV positive."

"But that's wonderful," she said, dumbfounded. "I thought he was tested, though."

"When you test positive, they administer a second test, which they did, but he never bothered to tell me the results — until yesterday. They were negative."

She stared at him, astonished at her own relief. "Why aren't you rejoicing?"

Crossing his arms, he said, "He wanted us to think he had the AIDS virus, so that we'd feel badly for him. Now I can kick him out."

"Oh, Troy, you don't want to throw him out. You want him to be someone he's not."

He dropped his belligerent stance and looked surprised. "Do you really think so?"

"Yeah."

When Dale wandered downstairs and into the kitchen, she said, "I heard the good news."

Dale grunted. "For now it's good. You never know."

"Oh, for crissakes," Troy said, snapping the newspaper open. "You're not getting any more sympathy from me."

As Fran took his and Sarah's jackets, Troy said, "Hi, Rhea, old girl. Ready for another game of cards?"

"Who are you?" Rhea asked, standing uncertainly in the living room.

"Your friend, Troy." He bent and kissed her cheek, then turned to Mimi. "And you look pretty good for someone who was nearly toast."

"Troy," Sarah protested. But Fran was grinning, and Mimi laughed.

"Swiss cheese is more like it." Mimi had seen the psychologist twice that week and hadn't screamed in the night since Wednesday.

They played sheepshead at the coffee table in the living room in front of a fire so that Mimi wouldn't have to leave the couch. Fran's mother couldn't remember to follow suit or what was trump. During the fourth hand, she excused herself and went to bed. Butch remained at Fran's feet.

"Shows what kind of company we are," Troy remarked. "I'd leave too, if I were her."

"God, I'll be glad when winter's over," Mimi said. "I want to feel warm again."

Fran looked at her. "Mimi's aunt asked her if she wanted to move to Florida and live with her."

"I wish I was in the land of cotton," Troy sang, trumping the last trick. "A lot of memories around here. Might not be a bad idea." He tossed the cards to Sarah to shuffle.

"This aunt is estranged from my parents. My dad calls her a dyke. Bob called her a dyke too, so maybe she is a lesbian." Mimi gave Fran a faint smile. "I hope so."

"It might be good for you to be shed of this place," Troy said.

"What do you think, Sarah?" Mimi asked.

"Troy's got a point. What do you say, Fran?"

"I'll miss her."

Mimi smiled fondly at Fran. "She promised to visit."

"We'll all spend the winters with you," Troy promised.

Sarah began dealing. Fran's son lived in Florida. Maybe she would take Rhea and go with Mimi. It made her feel somewhat desperate and more than a little lonely.

"Hey, cookie, watch where you're throwing my cards," Troy said, picking them off the floor.

"Sorry." Sarah felt Fran's gaze on her and met it. They were wary with each other, careful with what was said.

"How's Amelia these days?" Fran asked.

"Amelia's history," Troy said, "and Dale is miraculously cured. And so the world turns, or is it the worm?"

"What do you mean?" Fran and Mimi looked puzzled.

"Dale, who tested positive, now is negative. Amazing, isn't it?"

"It's wonderful," Fran said, staring at Troy.

Even Sarah wasn't sure what lay behind Troy's flippancy.

"What do you mean, 'Amelia's history'?" Mimi asked. She was propped up by two pillows. Her face was wan, her eyes huge pools of dark liquid.

"Tell them, Sarah," he urged.

"Nothing to tell," she said with an embarrassed shrug. "I'd say it's over, but I'm not sure it ever began."

Fran was looking out her mother's window at Meadow Manor. Houses were going up in the field next door. She turned back to the chair where her mother sat, bolt upright, staring at her strangely. "Mom, you can't wander off like that. It's too cold out, and this is a busy road. You could get hit."

"Why do you call me Mom? What are you doing here? Who are you?" her mother asked in a voice Fran had never heard.

The raw February wind outside settled in her chest. "I'm your daughter, Fran."

"I have no daughter called Fran. Don't bother me. Go away." The tone was sharp, unpleasant.

Hurt, she stared at her mother.

"Go, go," her mother said, flicking a knobby hand toward the door.

Fran went to find one of the staff. "Have you noticed any recent changes in my mother? She doesn't know me."

"She doesn't always know us, Fran." The woman touched her arm, offering comfort.

"Where did she think she was going when she went outside yesterday? Did you ask?" Fran wanted to hear that her mother had a destination.

"To her room. She said she had to use the bathroom."

She was terrified her mother would have to be moved from this nice place, that they wouldn't be able to handle her here.

"We'll keep an eye on her. Don't worry. Go back to her room, maybe she'll know who you are."

"Thanks," she said. "I should have brought the dog. She'd probably recognize him."

The room was dim when she reentered. Her mother lay in a small heap on the bed, asleep with her mouth open. Her hair was a snow-white jumble of flattened curls, her face pale and softly crumpled.

Bending, Fran kissed the velvety cheek and tiptoed from the room.

She drove to Mimi's apartment where she was

going to help her pack boxes. What little strength Mimi had was short-lived. Unlocking the door, Fran found her lying on the couch.

"I was just catching my breath," Mimi said, hauling herself to a sitting position.

"Tell me what you want packed and I'll do it. You stay there and talk to me." Slipping out of her jacket, she dropped it on a chair.

"How's your mom?"

"She didn't know me." Grabbing a tissue, she blew her nose angrily. "Sarah should be glad her mother died before she forgot who she was."

"I'm sorry, Fran." Mimi started to get up.

"That's okay. I'll be fine." She waved her back down. "She said I wasn't her daughter and told me to go away. And I was hurt as if she knew what she was saying. Pretty stupid, huh?"

"Not stupid at all," Mimi said. "You want something to cheer you up?"

"Like what?" she asked.

"Food, drink. I can't remember any jokes."

She laughed. "I'm going to miss you, Mimi, and yes, I'll have a drink. You can fix it while I stuff things into boxes." She got down on her knees. After moving into the Cape Cod, she'd told herself she'd never box again.

"I can't drink with you. I think I'd pass out." Mimi set a vodka and tonic on the coffee table. "Your face looks good. At first it hurt me to look at it, especially knowing I was the reason it happened."

"You can't blame yourself for what he did." The side of her face had healed, the colors changing and fading and disappearing in a matter of weeks. "Has your family given up trying to change your mind?"

"No." Mimi tucked one leg under herself and sat on the couch. "They're just like Bob. They get hold of something and they can't let it go, like a bulldog with a bone." She leaned back, her face wan and pinched looking.

"Does your side hurt still?"

"Some. It's nice of you-all to drive me to Florida."

"Practicing talking southern, woman?" Fran caught sight of Mimi's grin and matched it. "We're nice people. Besides, who would turn down a chance to go south in March?"

"I thought you might offer to help me move. I was going to ask you. I wasn't even surprised when Troy said he'd pull a trailer for me, but I sure didn't expect Sarah to want to go along. Did you?"

"Nope." She refused to be drawn into a conversation about Sarah.

"Are you going to visit Jay while you're in Florida?"

"There won't be time." He had phoned her after getting the lowdown on Christmas Day from Chelsey. She'd had to reassure him over and over that she was all right. "I'll call him."

XX

After closing the doors of the six-by-twelve U-Haul trailer and dropping the bar in its slot, Troy wiped his hands on his jeans. Mimi was taking very little with her. She'd sold her house and given the larger furniture to her sons, including the bed. She'd told Fran that she didn't want anything to remind her of Bob. The trailer was full of boxes and clothes, the microwave oven, a bookcase, a rocking chair, a desk, a stereo and CDs, the TV and VCR, things that didn't remind her directly of her marriage.

"Ready?" he asked. It was six A.M. Friday, March 1. Their goal today was to get south of Indianapolis. "We're going where the warm breezes blow, cookie," he said to Sarah as they climbed into his Explorer and drove away. Fran followed, driving Mimi's Blazer.

Sarah was more excited than she was willing to let him know.

"You should be riding with Fran," he said.

"Why? Don't you like my company?"

"You want to spend the rest of your life single?" They turned onto Highway 41, heading south. Troy stepped on the gas as if there was no trailer attached. "This baby's got power."

She asked her own question. "Did I hear you fighting with Dale last night?"

"He wanted to come. You know that. I can't afford to take him, and that's what it would amount to. I feed him, clean up after him, wash his clothes. I'm his goddamn wife."

"Now that he's not HIV positive you don't have to feel guilty about telling him to leave." She looked out the window at the still barren landscape — nothing blooming, nothing green with life except willow shoots. "I guess I don't understand your relationship. You talk about him like he's a pain in the ass, yet you keep him around. Why?"

"I'll tell you, Sarah, if you'll keep it quiet." He so seldom called her by her name that she glanced at him.

"That goes without saying, Troy."

"Do you know how many gay men grow old alone? I realize he's unreliable and sometimes dishonest and that he can't resist a handsome face. He's

209

not even a whole lot of fun. But he knows he can count on me — I'm his rock — so he stays or comes back."

"That's a good definition of codependency, Troy," she said, disturbed by his reasoning. "You're a good-looking, fun-loving man. Why be stuck with a loser?"

"When I find that elusive winner, I'll go with him."

"You don't think enough of yourself," she said on a hunch.

"Sure, I do. I'm a great fisherman, a wonderful lover, a good provider, and I'm handsome, to boot." He grinned at her. "How about a doughnut hole and some coffee?"

"Already? We ate breakfast less than an hour ago." They were passing Oshkosh. She dug into the food bag and poured him coffee out of the thermos.

They stopped for lunch at a rest stop on Interstate 65 south of 114 in Indiana. After a mad scramble for the restrooms, they found a picnic table under bare maples and shared turkey bologna sandwiches and potato chips.

"Already it feels warmer, don't you think?" Troy said.

Mimi laughed. "Kind of cool for a picnic."

There was a raw, wet chill in the air. Sarah hunched into her lightweight jacket and noticed Fran watching someone walking a dog. Butch was in BarkNoMore Kennel.

"Sorry we didn't bring him?"

Fran looked at her. "Yes and no. He'd cramp our

style, yet I hate leaving him at the kennel. You should have heard the racket. It was deafening. BarkNoMore, my ass."

"Why don't you ride with me this afternoon, Mimi?" Troy said.

"Do you mind if I lie in the backseat and take a nap? Maybe your suspension is less stiff than mine."

"The bouncing hurts her side," Fran explained.

"Whenever you want to stop, turn on your flashers," Sarah said, climbing behind the wheel of Mimi's Blazer. Fran had said she was tired of driving.

When they crossed the Wabash at Lafayette, Sarah asked Fran if she was going to move to Florida.

"God, no. I wouldn't live anywhere where there aren't laws protecting our rights."

"I thought, because Jay lives there and now Mimi —"

"I'll miss Mimi. I miss Jay. But I'm not going to move because they do. I can't make a life with either one." Fran turned her face to the window. "Why did you come on this trip, Sarah?"

Here was her opening. Sarah took a deep breath and jumped into it. "I thought I could help, and it was a chance to be with you again."

"Why did you leave me then?" Fran asked.

"Because I wanted a little freedom, because my mother died, because I was afraid I'd be bogged down taking care of yours." The last reason surprised even her. She threw a glance at Fran, who hadn't moved, and quickly returned her gaze to the road. Uncomfortable silence filled the Chevy.

Fran let out a sigh. "I figured the first two, that

you were feeling your mortality, that you needed a change. I didn't guess the last."

Sarah tried to explain, thinking out loud. "I joined a writing group, Fran. It's changed everything. I don't feel trapped anymore."

"Why would you? You're not with anyone."

"No. Listen, Fran. Writing is good therapy, at least for me. It frees me from any constraints. It was what I was looking for. I can be with someone again."

Fran remained turned toward the window and quiet as they entered the Indianapolis city limits. When she broke the silence, it was to comment on their surroundings.

They stopped for the night at a Holiday Inn on State Highway 46 near Columbus. They'd been on the road ten and a half hours. Mimi could barely walk. Carefully, she lay down on one of the double beds in the room the three women would share.

"We'll bring you room service," Troy promised, his hand on the doorknob.

"A burger and fries would be great." Her face was as white as it had been in the hospital. She covered her eyes with an arm.

"I think we'd better not drive such long stretches," Fran said on the way to the nearest McDonald's.

"We'll just get to Florida and have to turn back," Troy pointed out.

"We can do our sightseeing on the way instead," Sarah said. "You won't get to see Jay, though, Fran."

"I didn't expect to see him anyway." Fran shrugged. "I don't know about you two, but I'm really beat."

It was barely dark when Fran and Sarah went to bed. Troy protested, then decided to cruise Columbus alone. Mimi was asleep, having hardly touched the food they'd brought her.

"I'm worried. She looks so pale," Fran whispered, sliding between the sheets. She slept in an undershirt and panties as she always had.

Sarah had thought about who would sleep with whom. She'd been worried that Fran would decide to share a bed with Mimi. The sheets were cool against her legs and arms. She wore a nightshirt. Lying on her back, carefully not touching Fran, she stared at the shadows on the ceiling.

When she awakened in the night, Fran was tucked up against her. Her face was in Fran's hair, her arm flung carelessly over her ribs. She was sure Fran was awake. Testing her resistance, Sarah gathered her closer and carefully cupped a breast.

Fran moved away, muttering, "Don't."

She slid up behind her. "Why not?"

"Mimi," Fran whispered.

"Is that the only reason?"

"I don't do sex just for sex."

"I want to make love to you." She'd had no idea how much.

"No."

"Let me just hold you then."

"I don't think that's a good idea."

Sarah rolled onto her back. She would wait.

Mimi's aunt lived on Merritt Island in a double trailer in what was once a grapefruit grove. To get there from the mainland they crossed the Indian River. The island was separated from Cape Kennedy on the other side by the Banana River. Mimi's aunt had told her that from their porch they could see the space shuttle once it was launched.

When Fran and Sarah drove into the trailer park, followed by the Explorer, it was like driving into summer. Grapefruit bowed the branches of the trees, flowers bloomed, the grass was a green carpet. It was evening, the air heady with blossoms and thick with salty humidity and heat.

The screen door slammed behind two women as Sarah and the others got out of the two vehicles. One of the women said, "We were worried. It took you so long. But never mind, now you're here. Come on inside. Which one of you is Fran?"

Fran stepped forward with a smile. "I am. And this is Sarah and Troy."

"Let me stand and smell this air for a minute. We haven't smelled anything for months. It's been too cold," Troy said.

"I'm Mimi's Aunt Rose and this is Lynn. Come here, honey," she said to Mimi. "You look beat. You need some sun to brighten those cheeks." Putting an arm around Mimi, she led her onto the porch.

The two women's large frames overflowed their shorts and T-shirts. Their graying hair was cut short. Lynn held the door open for the bedraggled company. The porch was furnished for comfort. Books and magazines lay on the tabletops. Half-finished drinks were also evident.

"Can I get you anything?" Lynn asked. "We're having gin and tonic."

"I think a drink might be in order," Rose said, eyeing Fran.

"I won't turn one down." Troy sat on one of the canvas chairs. "This is great." Insects hummed beyond the screens.

"Thanks. Can I help?" Fran asked.

"No, honey. You just stay here on the porch with your friends," Rose said, disappearing with Lynn into the house.

They returned a few minutes later with drinks and snacks. Sarah was watching them as they exchanged glances. She took a swig of her drink and waited.

"Look," Rose said, sitting down facing Fran. "We got a phone call just before you arrived. We thought we'd give you a little time to collect yourself. It was from Meadow Manor. Your mother wandered away last night. She suffered from hypothermia and is in the hospital, but they don't think she's in any danger."

Fran stood up. "Where's the phone?"

Sarah followed her into the other room and listened to the conversation. When Fran hung up, Sarah said, "I'll fly home with you tomorrow."

"She's not going to be able to stay at Meadow Manor, Sarah. I'll have to find a more secure place."

"Maybe, maybe not. Do you want me to call the airlines?"

"No. She's not in any danger. They phoned my brother."

* * * * *

"We've got three bedrooms and the sleeper sofa," Rose had said, after Mimi had gone to bed in one of the rooms.

"I'll take the sofa," Troy had volunteered.

Now Fran lay next to Sarah in a double bed in the third bedroom and stared at the ceiling fan turning slowly overhead. The hum of insects had grown louder with the deepening darkness. Frogs chunked from somewhere close. Traffic whirred past on the nearby highway. "You asleep?"

"Nope. I'm so sorry about Rhea, Fran. We all are. Growing old sucks," Sarah said with vehemence.

"I know. I'd like it if you held me now." She laid her head on Sarah's shoulder and closed her eyes as Sarah put an arm around her. This was how they had lain before getting up in the mornings when they lived together.

Sarah's breath tickled Fran's forehead. "I'm sorry I said I didn't want to get stuck with taking care of your mother. I don't know where it came from. I certainly didn't mean it."

"Yes, you did." She put a finger against Sarah's lips. "It's okay. I understand. I'd have felt the same way."

"But I care about your mother, and I love you."

She wiped Sarah's cheeks with her fingers. "Why the tears?"

"You should hate me and you don't."

"Mmm." She inhaled Sarah's odor, so distinctive, so familiar. "I've seen the results of that kind of hate. Bob's dead; Mimi will probably never be the same. You know what I want to do right now?"

It had been so long, yet Fran hadn't forgotten the many ways they made love. Always, they began with kissing, the gentle brushing of lips across cheeks and eyes and necks and finally the taste of soft mouths, the teasing of tongues. Then Fran was frantic with desire, with lust, knowing from Sarah's touch that she felt the same urgent need. Their hands moved quickly between each other's legs, and they laughed quietly at the readiness there. Sarah pushed Fran on her back and covered her with her length. Her mouth was on Fran's breasts, her fingers inside, and Fran wrapped her legs around her, forcing her to stop. They thrust at each other, grunting.

Rolling onto their sides, face-to-face, mouth-to-mouth, one leg apiece crooked upward, they stroked each other and moaned softly with pleasure. As Sarah lifted herself, turned head-to-tail, and went down on her, Fran drew Sarah's hips toward her, tasting the need, feeling the spasms that quickly followed. Sarah's tongue flitted across her, her fingers deep inside, and she too convulsed in climax.

After, they lay still while their hearts thudded in unison and their breathing steadied. Fran pulled the sheet over them.

Sarah cleared her throat. "I guess we haven't forgotten how."

Fran was experiencing a strange mix of feelings: disgust, desire, a need to run, a wish to curl up against Sarah. "No. How was it with Amelia?" she asked.

"What?" Sarah shrugged. "Nothing like this."

She edged toward the side of the bed, and Sarah moved with her.

"You're backing away from me. Don't do it, Fran."

Turning toward the wall, Fran felt Sarah scoot up

against her backside. Sleep lay heavy on her, dissolving her resistance. She thought of her mother, felt briefly guilty, then decided to deal with everything tomorrow.

They drove straight through on the way home, taking turns at the wheel, stopping only to eat and pee. They had run out of vacation time. Mimi and Fran had cried at their departure. Fran had been quiet since, and Sarah assumed that she missed Mimi and was not looking forward to dealing with the problem of her mother. Troy was snoring in the backseat, while Fran was stretched out in the passenger seat next to her. They were north of Milwaukee on their last leg before home.

"I'll come with you to see your mother, if you like," she offered.

"Thanks," Fran said. "I appreciate that."

"What do you think about my suggestion?" They had made love every night in Florida as if they were starved for it.

"What does Troy say?"

"About what?" he asked. "Where are we?"

"Near West Bend," Sarah said. "About my moving in with Fran."

"I think you should both move in with me." He sat up. His cheeks were ruddy, his dark hair tousled.

Fran popped her seat upright. Her face was bright from too much sun. She ran fingers through her hair. "You'd have to buy a bigger house."

"Hey, good idea. Why don't we all buy a house together," he suggested. Leaning forward, he stuck his head between the seats and put a hand on each of their shoulders. "Actually, I think you two deserve each other."

Fran found her mother sitting in the chair in her room, staring out the window. Sarah waited in the doorway.

"Mom?"

Her mother turned with a puzzled expression.

"How are you, Mom? I went to Florida for a week. I heard that you walked away from here on a cold night and had to go to the hospital."

"What's your name again, honey?"

"Fran."

"And your friend there? What's her name?"

"That's Sarah. Mom, I'm your daughter."

Her mother was shaking her head. Fran could see her struggling with confusion. "I don't know you. What's your name?"

Sarah stepped forward. "Want to go out for dinner, Rhea?"

"Oh, I'd love that." She lowered her voice to a whisper. "Don't tell them, though. They won't let me go anywhere."

"As long as you're with us, they will," Sarah said.

Fran stood aside, while Sarah got her mother's coat out of the closet and helped her into it. She followed them out of the room and down the hall toward the evening light. Her mother was holding Sarah's arm. She felt a twinge of jealousy. She was only another person in her mother's life, no longer her daughter. You asshole, she thought, hurrying ahead to hold open the doors. It apparently made no difference to her mother. Fran was the one who cared.

Epilogue

The boat rocked on the passing wake of another, and Troy waved a fist at it. Beating down out of a nearly cloudless sky, the July sun pricked Fran's skin like needles. She smeared more sunblock on herself and held it out to Sarah, who stood with her back to the wheel, casting.

Sarah shook her head.

"You're burning," Fran warned, tossing the bottle past her to Troy.

"She's right," he said.

"Okay." Sarah reeled in and set her rod down. "When is Ron coming up?" she asked Troy.

"This weekend." Ron had replaced Dale, who'd left Troy for another pretty face.

"Does he like to fish?" Sarah asked.

"He says he does. I'll leave him if he doesn't."

"I haven't divorced Fran. She'd rather read than fish." Sarah gave Fran a white grin.

Fran smiled, enjoying their banter. A heron was stalking minnows in the shallows. High overhead an eagle circled. Two loons swam near shore, their baby between them. Midafternoon they would return to their cabin, where Butch waited, and go for a swim. Her book lay in her lap, her fishing pole at her feet.

This wonderful week would end. They would return home to the real world, where her mother lived in a facility with locks on the doors and didn't know her own daughter. She herself would start another job in the accounting department where she worked. The pay wasn't as good as driving the delivery trucks, but there were, at least, opportunities for advancement.

"Fran? You're not bored, are you?" Sarah asked. Her story had been accepted. She had said that being published was the icing on the cake, that the cake was the two of them together again.

Fran squinted up at Sarah. "Having a good time?"

"Never better." The sun was at Sarah's back, turning her honey-blonde hair into a bright halo. Her eyes glowed. "It should always be like this."

"We'd take it for granted." Fran had happily settled for contentment.

Troy shouted, "Get the net, cookie. There's a monster on my line."

222

About the Author

Jackie Calhoun is the author of *Abby's Passion, Woman in the Mirror, Outside the Flock, Tamarack Creek*, and *Off Season*, published by Bella Books; ten romances by Naiad Press; and *Crossing the Center Line*, printed by Windstorm Creative Ltd. Calhoun lives in Northeast Wisconsin.

Publications from
BELLA BOOKS, INC.
The best in contemporary lesbian fiction

P.O. Box 10543, Tallahassee, FL 32302
Phone: 800-729-4992
www.bellabooks.com

DAWN OF CHANGE by Gerri Hill. 240 pp. Susan ran away to find peace in remote Kings Canyon—then she met Shawn . . .   ISBN 1-59493-011-2 $12.95

DOWN THE RABBIT HOLE by Lynne Jamneck. 240 pp. Is a killer holding a grudge against FBI Agent Samantha Skellar?   ISBN 1-59493-012-0 $12.95

SEASONS OF THE HEART by Jackie Calhoun. 240 pp. Overwhelmed, Sara saw only one way out—leaving . . .   ISBN 1-59493-030-9 $12.95

TURNING THE TABLES by Jessica Thomas. 240 pp. The 2nd Alex Peres Mystery. *From ghosties and ghoulies and long leggity beasties* . . .   ISBN 1-59493-009-0 $12.95

FOR EVERY SEASON by Frankie Jones. 240 pp. Andi, who is investigating a 65-year-old murder meets Janice, a charming district attorney . . .   ISBN 1-59493-010-4 $12.95

LOVE ON THE LINE by Laura DeHart Young. 240 pp. Kay leaves a younger woman behind to go on a mission to Alaska . . . will she regret it?   ISBN 1-59493-008-2 $12.95

UNDER THE SOUTHERN CROSS by Claire McNab. 200 pp. Lee, an American travel agent, goes down under and meets Australian Alex, and the sparks fly under the Southern Cross.   ISBN 1-59493-029-5 $12.95

SUGAR by Karin Kallmaker. 240 pp. Three women want sugar from Sugar, who can't make up her mind.   ISBN 1-59493-001-5 $12.95

FALL GUY by Claire McNab. 200 pp. 16th Detective Inspector Carol Ashton Mystery.
                                                                        ISBN 1-59493-000-7 $12.95

ONE SUMMER NIGHT by Gerri Hill. 232 pp. Johanna swore to never fall in love again—but then she met the charming Kelly . . .   ISBN 1-59493-007-4 $12.95

TALK OF THE TOWN TOO by Saxon Bennett. 181 pp. Second in the series about wild and fun loving friends.   ISBN 1-931513-77-5 $12.95

LOVE SPEAKS HER NAME by Laura DeHart Young. 170 pp. Love and friendship, desire and intrigue, spark this exciting sequel to *Forever and the Night.*
                                                                        ISBN 1-59493-002-3 $12.95

TO HAVE AND TO HOLD by Peggy J. Herring. 184 pp. By finally letting down her defenses, will Dorian be opening herself to a devastating betrayal?
                                                                        ISBN 1-59493-005-8 $12.95

WILD THINGS by Karin Kallmaker. 228 pp. Dutiful daughter Faith has met the perfect man. There's just one problem: she's in love with his sister.   ISBN 1-931513-64-3 $12.95

SHARED WINDS by Kenna White. 216 pp. Can Emma rebuild more than just Lanny's marina? ISBN 1-59493-006-6 $12.95

THE UNKNOWN MILE by Jaime Clevenger. 253 pp. Kelly's world is getting more and more complicated every moment. ISBN 1-931513-57-0 $12.95

TREASURED PAST by Linda Hill. 189 pp. A shared passion for antiques leads to love. ISBN 1-59493-003-1 $12.95

SIERRA CITY by Gerri Hill. 284 pp. Chris and Jesse cannot deny their growing attraction . . . ISBN 1-931513-98-8 $12.95

ALL THE WRONG PLACES by Karin Kallmaker. 174 pp. Sex and the single girl—Brandy is looking for love and usually she finds it. Karin Kallmaker's first *After Dark* erotic novel. ISBN 1-931513-76-7 $12.95

WHEN THE CORPSE LIES A Motor City Thriller by Therese Szymanski. 328 pp. Butch bad-girl Brett Higgins is used to waking up next to beautiful women she hardly knows. Problem is, this one's dead. ISBN 1-931513-74-0 $12.95

GUARDED HEARTS by Hannah Rickard. 240 pp. Someone's reminding Alyssa about her secret past, and then she becomes the suspect in a series of burglaries. ISBN 1-931513-99-6 $12.95

ONCE MORE WITH FEELING by Peggy J. Herring. 184 pp. Lighthearted, loving, romantic adventure. ISBN 1-931513-60-0 $12.95

TANGLED AND DARK A Brenda Strange Mystery by Patty G. Henderson. 240 pp. When investigating a local death, Brenda finds two possible killers—one diagnosed with Multiple Personality Disorder. ISBN 1-931513-75-9 $12.95

WHITE LACE AND PROMISES by Peggy J. Herring. 240 pp. Maxine and Betina realize sex may not be the most important thing in their lives. ISBN 1-931513-73-2 $12.95

UNFORGETTABLE by Karin Kallmaker. 288 pp. Can Rett find love with the cheerleader who broke her heart so many years ago? ISBN 1-931513-63-5 $12.95

HIGHER GROUND by Saxon Bennett. 280 pp. A delightfully complex reflection of the successful, high society lives of a small group of women. ISBN 1-931513-69-4 $12.95

LAST CALL A Detective Franco Mystery by Baxter Clare. 240 pp. Frank overlooks all else to try to solve a cold case of two murdered children . . . ISBN 1-931513-70-8 $12.95

ONCE UPON A DYKE: NEW EXPLOITS OF FAIRY-TALE LESBIANS by Karin Kallmaker, Julia Watts, Barbara Johnson & Therese Szymanski. 320 pp. You've never read fairy tales like these before! From Bella After Dark. ISBN 1-931513-71-6 $14.95

FINEST KIND OF LOVE by Diana Tremain Braund. 224 pp. Can Molly and Carolyn stop clashing long enough to see beyond their differences? ISBN 1-931513-68-6 $12.95

DREAM LOVER by Lyn Denison. 188 pp. A soft, sensuous, romantic fantasy. ISBN 1-931513-96-1 $12.95

NEVER SAY NEVER by Linda Hill. 224 pp. A classic love story . . . where rules aren't the only things broken. ISBN 1-931513-67-8 $12.95

PAINTED MOON by Karin Kallmaker. 214 pp. Stranded together in a snowbound cabin, Jackie and Leah's lives will never be the same. ISBN 1-931513-53-8 $12.95

WIZARD OF ISIS by Jean Stewart. 240 pp. Fifth in the exciting Isis series. ISBN 1-931513-71-4 $12.95

WOMAN IN THE MIRROR by Jackie Calhoun. 216 pp. Josey learns to love again, while her niece is learning to love women for the first time. ISBN 1-931513-78-3 $12.95

SUBSTITUTE FOR LOVE by Karin Kallmaker. 200 pp. When Holly and Reyna meet the combination adds up to pure passion. But what about tomorrow? ISBN 1-931513-62-7 $12.95

GULF BREEZE by Gerri Hill. 288 pp. Could Carly really be the woman Pat has always been searching for? ISBN 1-931513-97-X $12.95

THE TOMSTOWN INCIDENT by Penny Hayes. 184 pp. Caught between two worlds, Eloise must make a decision that will change her life forever. ISBN 1-931513-56-2 $12.95

MAKING UP FOR LOST TIME by Karin Kallmaker. 240 pp. Discover delicious recipes for romance by the undisputed mistress. ISBN 1-931513-61-9 $12.95

THE WAY LIFE SHOULD BE by Diana Tremain Braund. 173 pp. With which woman will Jennifer find the true meaning of love? ISBN 1-931513-66-X $12.95

BACK TO BASICS: A BUTCH/FEMME ANTHOLOGY edited by Therese Szymanski—from Bella After Dark. 324 pp. ISBN 1-931513-35-X $14.95

SURVIVAL OF LOVE by Frankie J. Jones. 236 pp. What will Jody do when she falls in love with her best friend's daughter? ISBN 1-931513-55-4 $12.95

LESSONS IN MURDER by Claire McNab. 184 pp. 1st Detective Inspector Carol Ashton Mystery. ISBN 1-931513-65-1 $12.95

DEATH BY DEATH by Claire McNab. 167 pp. 5th Denise Cleever Thriller. ISBN 1-931513-34-1 $12.95

CAUGHT IN THE NET by Jessica Thomas. 188 pp. A wickedly observant story of mystery, danger, and love in Provincetown. ISBN 1-931513-54-6 $12.95

DREAMS FOUND by Lyn Denison. Australian Riley embarks on a journey to meet her birth mother . . . and gains not just a family, but the love of her life. ISBN 1-931513-58-9 $12.95

A MOMENT'S INDISCRETION by Peggy J. Herring. 154 pp. Jackie is torn between her better judgment and the overwhelming attraction she feels for Valerie. ISBN 1-931513-59-7 $12.95

IN EVERY PORT by Karin Kallmaker. 224 pp. Jessica has a woman in every port. Will meeting Cat change all that? ISBN 1-931513-36-8 $12.95

TOUCHWOOD by Karin Kallmaker. 240 pp. Rayann loves Louisa. Louisa loves Rayann. Can the decades between their ages keep them apart? ISBN 1-931513-37-6 $12.95

WATERMARK by Karin Kallmaker. 248 pp. Teresa wants a future with a woman whose heart has been frozen by loss. Sequel to *Touchwood*. ISBN 1-931513-38-4 $12.95

EMBRACE IN MOTION by Karin Kallmaker. 240 pp. Has Sarah found lust or love? ISBN 1-931513-39-2 $12.95

ONE DEGREE OF SEPARATION by Karin Kallmaker. 232 pp. Sizzling small town romance between Marian, the town librarian, and the new girl from the big city. ISBN 1-931513-30-9 $12.95

CRY HAVOC A Detective Franco Mystery by Baxter Clare. 240 pp. A dead hustler with a headless rooster in his lap sends Lt. L.A. Franco headfirst against Mother Love. ISBN 1-931513931-7 $12.95